Chasing Fire

BOOKS WRITTEN AND ILLUSTRATED BY EARL FLECK

CHASING FIRE: DANGER IN CANOE COUNTRY (2002)

CHASING BEARS: A CANOE COUNTRY ADVENTURE (1999)

Chasing Fire

DANGER IN
CANOE COUNTRY

WRITTEN AND ILLUSTRATED

BY

EARL FLECK

HOLY COW! PRESS · 2002 · DULUTH, MINNESOTA

First Printing, 2002
10 9 8 7 6 5 4 3 2 1

Library of Congress Cataloging-in-Publication Data

Fleck, Earl, 1950-
Chasing fire : danger in canoe country / Earl Fleck.
p.   cm.
Summary: Thirteen-year-old Danny and his family
go on a challenging camping and canoeing trip from
Minnesota into Canada, planning to rendezvous with
Danny's older fire fighter brother along the way.
ISBN 0-930100-53-0
[1. Canoes and canoeing—Fiction. 2. Camping—Fiction.
3. Forest fires—Fiction. 4. Boundary Waters Canoe Area (Minn.)—Fiction.
5. Ontario—Fiction. 6. Canada—Fiction.]
I. Title.

PZ7.F59863 Ck   2002
[Fic]—dc21   2002017162

Publisher's Address:
Holy Cow! Press
Post Office Box 3170
Mount Royal Station
Duluth, Minnesota 55803

Holy Cow! Press books are distributed to the trade by Consortium
Book Sales & Distribution, 1045 Westgate Drive, Saint Paul,
Minnesota 55114-1065.

For Connie and Leah, true campers.

Contents

chapter one

FIRE DANGER HIGH

C hased by the raging fire, Danny Forester ran headlong through the campsite toward the lake. Hot flames jumped treetop to treetop overhead, lighting up the night sky. Black smoke choking—red deer dashing. Harder and harder he ran—legs aching—lungs bursting.

"Run, Danny! Run!" He could hear Mike, his big brother, shouting from behind him. "Run into the lake!"

Sparks all around—flames—flaming branches falling—trees exploding from the heat—lungs burning—black smoke choking.

"Run, Danny! Run!"

Zigzagging pell-mell over the ground—dodging flames—leaping boulders—tripping—falling—crying out—afraid to look back.

"Get up, Danny! Run!"

Heat searing—smoke choking—voice screaming—adrenaline pumping—an inferno of fear—until at last the lake—the cool wet wonderful lake!

"Dive, Danny! Dive deep!"

Careening over the rocks. Splash! He dove deep—swimming underwater—legs kicking—arms pulling—lungs bursting. Touching bottom then up and up and up—searching like fire for oxygen. Up and up and up—breaking the surface into the night air—into the burning wilderness night air. Eyes open—voice screaming, "Mike! No!"

Mike on fire! Mike on fire, with a burning wood canoe on his shoulders, running into the lake! Mike on fire, running into the lake, trying to save their flaming red wood canoe! Mike on fire!

·   ·   ·

Danny sat up in the dark with a start, face all wet, breathing hard, confused. *Where am I? Where am I?* He held his breath and listened for a moment, letting his eyes adjust to the dark. Then he remembered. He was in a tent with his family at a campsite on Lake Agnes in the Boundary Waters Canoe Area Wilderness in far northern Minnesota. The wetness on his face was sweat. And he realized—the dream had found him again—the Mike-on-fire dream.

He wiped his brow with the sleeve of his sweatshirt. As his beating heart quieted down, he could hear the rhythmic deep-sleep breathing of his mother and little sister beside him, but no sound of his father. He looked out through the screen window of the tent. There, maybe fifty feet away, he could see the dark silhouette of his father, sitting hunched over on a campsite log next to the glowing fire. Danny unzipped the door to the tent, slipped on his sneakers and padded over to the campfire like some kind of nocturnal animal curious about the light.

"Hey, camper, what're you doing up?" Hank Forester handed his thirteen-year-old son a hot cup of cocoa. It was near midnight.

"I... I had the Mike dream again."

"I see," Hank nodded. He motioned for Danny to sit next to him on the log. "You mean the fire dream?"

"Yeah." Danny took a sip of cocoa.

"With the burning wood canoe?"

"Yeah, just like I told you before."

Hank paused for a moment, sipping his own cup of cocoa. "What happened to Mike was pretty scary for all of us, wasn't it?"

"Yeah, I guess so. But... but Mike is okay now, so I don't understand why I keep having this nightmare. I just wish he were here with us on this trip. We could use him."

"I know, Danny. I miss Mike, too. This is the first summer he hasn't come with us." Hank stirred the fire with a long stick.

. . .

Mike was Danny's nineteen-year-old brother. He had started college the last school year, but had quit in April to join a hotshot forest fire crew in Colorado. One day Mike hoped to become a smokejumper. He was big and strong and athletic, a great guy to have on a canoe trip. He could paddle and portage and chop wood and fish all day long, nonstop, and lead songs around the campfire at night. College was just too boring for him—sitting at a computer working out engineering equations was not his idea of fun. He wanted action, excitement—and danger.

This year the dry season had come early to the West, so Mike simply took off for Colorado one day, loading his belongings into the back of his pickup truck. Hank and Maddy Forester, his parents, were not happy with his decision to drop out of school. Maddy, especially, argued with Mike long distance over the phone, but eventually she gave into his wanderlust for adventure. All spring she and Hank followed the forest fire news stories on television, even the cable news and weather channels. Daily they checked the firefighting web sites on the Internet. Then tragedy struck.

The first week in May, Mike and his crew were working a wildfire called the Hungry Gulch Fire in the mountains of Utah—hot, exhausting, mean work. With shovels and chainsaws they dug a firebreak and cleared out the oak brush below a ridge running parallel to the fire. All the firefighters carried an equipment pack containing their gear, including a laminated foil fire shelter nicknamed "shake 'n' bake"—basically a big foil bag a firefighter could crawl into to escape being burned alive if a fire should somehow overtake him or her. At first it seemed like the flames were under control. Then the wind changed. A series of flare-ups in the juniper trees signaled trouble. The crew chief saw it first—the flame front turning into a blowup. He hollered for everyone to drop their packs, grab their fire shelters and run to the top of the ridge. They had trained for this kind of emergency.

Chased by the fire, Mike ran hard for the ridge, jumping over boulders and fallen trees, losing his hardhat. Like a bull elk he ran harder and harder, sensing the hot death at his back. Through his yellow fire shirt he could feel the intense burning heat on his skin. He had heard about vaporized fuel, hot gases, moving uphill ahead of the flames, then igniting and exploding in a fireball, hitting firefighters with a shock wave, knocking them down and trapping them where they fell, smothering their lungs. Smart Mike gambled. Finding a low spot in the terrain, he hurriedly opened his fire shelter and crawled into it face down, sealing the opening of the shelter tight against the ground. He knew that no matter how hot it got in the shake 'n' bake, it would be ten or twenty times hotter outside.

He survived the fiery blast of exploding gases by protecting his airways and holding his breath. Others were not so lucky. Three of his fellow crewmembers died in the Hungry Gulch Fire. Mike was evacuated by helicopter to a nearby hospital. There, he was treated for severe burns to his back and the back of his head and neck. The heat had singed all the hair off his head.

While in the hospital, two investigators from the U.S. Forest Service interviewed Mike about the fire. He told them what he could remember hearing and seeing in the smoke and confusion of the firestorm. They tape-recorded his statement.

Hank and Maddy flew out to Utah to bring Mike home. He returned on the plane with his mother, his head and neck bandaged. Hank drove his truck back to Minneapolis where the family lived. By the time Hank returned, Maddy had already taken Mike to the burn specialists in St. Paul. Luckily, he had suffered only second-degree burns and would heal with time and treatment. His lungs were clean.

Maddy put her foot down—no more firefighting for Mike. For a month he convalesced at home, brooding about the Hungry Gulch Fire. He seemed angry and impatient with his family, and spent his days going for long runs and lifting weights. Danny sensed his brother's restlessness, especially as they listened to the news reports of increased fire danger in the Boundary Waters Canoe Area Wilderness, or BWCAW, as it is known. No wilderness region was more important to Mike than the Boundary Waters.

Near the end of May a large envelope arrived in the mail for Mike. It contained a letter from the western regional director of the Forest Service, along with a typed transcript of Mike's statement to the investigators. The letter instructed him to sign his statement and return it to the director. That evening, he sat at the kitchen table with his parents.

"I could have saved those guys, that's what I should have told those investigators." Mike hung his head, his broad muscular shoulders nearly as wide as the table. Danny listened from the family room.

"Mike, the deaths of your friends were not your fault. You did exactly what your crew chief told you to do. You can't go on blaming yourself like this." Maddy spoke softly, placing her hand on her son's big forearm.

"You and Dad don't understand. You weren't there. I was bigger, stronger, smarter... better than any of those guys. I should have figured out some way to help them up that ridge." He threw his pen down on the table. "Why? Why them and not me?" He fought back tears.

"Mike, I've seen this kind of self-blame in others, when I worked in the Emergency Room at the hospital. Big tough guys... cops... firefighters... paramedics... who did everything they were trained to do and told to do, but still someone died. It happens, terrible as it is, you can't save everybody." Maddy rubbed her hand on his back. "You didn't even have the opportunity to attend their funerals. It says here that a memorial service is planned for September in Denver. I think it would help for you to attend this service."

Mike shrugged his shoulders and looked away.

Hank spoke up. "Mike, you know when you gather firewood at a campsite... sometimes you come across what looks like a nice piece of birch wood, but you pick it up off the forest floor and discover it's all rotted inside... all that's left is an empty tube of white birch bark. That's how it is with your sadness and anger and grief... if you hold it in, you'll rot inside like a piece of birch wood."

"Well, what am I supposed to do... I am angry!" Mike snapped at his father.

Danny startled at the intensity of Mike's emotions. He felt his nine-year-old sister, Rachel, pressed against his side, trembling. Sometimes big Mike's anger could frighten both of them. He signaled his little sister to keep quiet as they both listened in on the kitchen conversation.

Maddy held the letter in her hands. "In the last paragraph it says that crisis counselors are available for the survivors of the fire. There's a phone number you can call. Perhaps..."

"Geez! Now you're treating me like I'm some kind of a nut case. I don't need any crisis counseling. I can handle this myself... in my own way." Mike pushed his chair hard away from the table, stood up and stormed red-faced out of the room like a wild animal breaking out of a cage.

A few days later, Hank and Maddy returned from grocery shopping to find Mike loading his pick-up truck with his clothes, sleeping bag and fire fighting gear. Danny witnessed the argument out on the front lawn.

"I've signed on with a crew up north, the Boundary Waters district. And don't try to stop me. If there's going to be a Boundary Waters fire, I want to be there, fighting it."

"Michael, I absolutely forbid you to fight fires." Maddy reached for his arm. Mike pulled away. "Hank! Do something to stop him!" But Hank remained silent. He just stood, hands in his pockets, and watched as Mike drove angrily away. Maddy stomped into the house, slamming the door. Hank sat quietly on the front porch late into the night. Danny and Rachel stayed out of their way. But that night, Danny experienced the first of his Mike-on-fire dreams.

.   .   .

That was the first week in June. Since then, Danny had observed that things seemed a bit tense between his parents. Maddy would go off to the University of Minnesota in the morning, where she taught Emergency Room medicine. She was trained as an E.R. physician. Hank would spend long hours in his painting studio. He had the summer off from his art instructor position at a local community college. They didn't spend much time together. But despite this friction, they still found time to plan the annual Forester family canoe trip, this year a July trip, right at the peak of the blueberry season. Some Minnesota families were hockey families or soccer families. The Foresters were a camping family—a wilderness canoe camping family.

For this trip, Danny was recognized as his mother's chief first aid assistant. Together they cleaned up the first aid kit, replenishing the supplies used up in last year's adventure. Sitting at the kitchen table one evening, a week before the trip, they reviewed their wilderness first aid procedures. Danny noticed that his mother seemed distracted or disinterested. He had a thought that perhaps she didn't want to go on this trip. "Are you sure you really want to go with us this year?" he risked the question. "Dad and I can go by ourselves. We'll be okay."

"I'm sorry, Danny, if I gave you the impression that I don't want to go. I do want to. I'm just worried about Mike. I don't like what happened to him in Utah and I don't like us being out of communication for a week, with no way for Mike to reach us if something bad happens." She folded a triangle bandage as she talked. "Maybe I've just finally seen too much tragedy down at the E.R. Danny, I've seen the very worst. Believe me, I know what terrible burns can look like."

"But we'll be careful. We know how to camp." Danny tried to reassure his mother. "You can't hold us back just because of all the terrible stuff you've seen down at the Emergency Room."

"I know, Danny, you're right. Besides, I'd worry more about you and your father out on the trail alone than if I were with you, especially after what happened last year."

"Okay, then, you're coming with us."

"Yes, and gladly." Maddy Forester nodded her head and tousled Danny's sandy-colored hair. "I'll send a letter to Mike at the firefighter base camp telling him what days we'll be on the trail and what lakes we'll be camped on. Maybe he can meet up with us somewhere in the Boundary Waters?"

"Yes!" Danny pumped his right fist.

The next day, working beside his father, Danny helped ready the camping equipment. This year Hank taught him how to sharpen the axe and clean the saw blade. They even bought a new tent to replace the old tent destroyed in a storm on last year's trip. Together with Rachel they painted Native American pictograph images on the paddle blades. On Maddy's paddle they decided to paint a turtle. Rachel wanted a thunderbird symbol because she liked bald eagles. Danny still had his paddle from last year, with its bear pictograph painted in black. Hank had been given a new paddle for his birthday this year. On its wide blade, he painted the figure of a canoe with five paddlers and a flag.

There was never any question about Hank Forester going on the trip. He grew up in the canoe country of northwestern Ontario and he remained a Canadian citizen. The annual family canoe trip was a necessity for him, like food or air to breathe. He would never skip the canoe trip. Even if no one else would go along, he would go alone. "It's *the call of the wild* in my blood," he told Danny as he oiled the blade of the axe.

That night the four campers, Danny, Rachel, Maddy and Hank, studied their Boundary Waters maps, planning a route for this summer's trip. They all wanted a route with few portages, so they decided on Lake Lac La Croix. Next they planned their meals for the trip. Everyone voted for trail pizza, chili-mac with cornbread and Hudson Bay stew. Hank's favorite breakfast, rice-and-raisins, got voted down. Maddy hoped they'd find enough blueberries for her to bake a pie on the trail.

Then, the night before the trip, Mike called long distance from Ely, Minnesota. Ely was the small town that was the last point of civilization before entering the western BWCAW.

Danny answered the phone. Hank and Maddy were out buy-
ing the last of the trail food and some mosquito repellent.

Mike shouted into the phone against the background
noise of a truck engine. "Tell Mom and Dad there's a fire on
Crane Lake. We've had a bunch of little fires to snuff out, but
this one looks like the real thing—a fire we can be proud to
fight. My crew is heading up there tonight."

Danny could sense the excitement in Mike's voice. "Did
you get Mom's letter telling you about our route?" he asked.

"Yeah, that's why I'm calling." Mike sounded almost out
of breath. "We should have this fire out in no time—two days
max. Tell Mom I'll try to meet up with you guys on Iron Lake
on your sixth night out. Okay?"

"Where on Iron Lake?" Danny didn't want to miss any
important piece of information. He knew his mother would
question him for the details of Mike's call.

"I don't know. I gotta' go. My crew's leaving. Just find a
campsite and I'll find you." Mike hung up the phone with a
hard click.

When Hank and Maddy returned home, Danny told them
about Mike's phone call. Hank explained that Crane Lake was
a big lake just to the west of the BWCAW. In the Boundary
Waters, there were no roads or lake cabins or resorts allowed.
It was a wilderness area reserved for canoe camping. But Crane
Lake was populated with resorts, fishing camps and cabins.
The firefighters would be fighting not only to save the nation-
al forest, but to save private property as well. Without saying
it, Danny knew that Mike would be in the thick of the fight.

While they packed out their food and equipment for the
trip, Maddy kept the television on in the kitchen, listening
for news of the Crane Lake fire. At midnight, Hank and
Danny loaded up the Forester's old red Chevy Suburban,
packs inside, two canoes on top. Then, just before one o'clock
in the morning, they left for the six-hour drive north from

Minneapolis to Ely, Minnesota. Danny and Rachel slept in the back of the truck. Hank and Maddy took turns driving, listening to the radio for any report about the fire.

Danny woke up at seven in the morning and looked out the side window of the Suburban. A big red and yellow sign in front of the U.S. Forest Service ranger station read: FIRE DANGER HIGH.

They had stopped at the ranger station to pick up their BWCAW camping permit. The ranger had them watch a videotape explaining the park rules, and a second video about fire safety. Like all campers, the Foresters had to answer a series of questions to show that they understood the rules. No cans or bottles for food or beverages. No soap in the lakes. No feeding the bears. And this year, because of the increased fire danger, open campfires would be allowed only from seven o'clock in the evening until midnight.

Despite Maddy pressing him for details, the ranger had little to report about the Crane Lake fire except to speculate that if the wind stayed down, it should be under control by nightfall that day. A quick breakfast in Ely and a drive farther north, up a winding logging road called the Echo Trail, took the Foresters to the start of their trip—the Moose River to Lake Agnes, where they camped for their first night on the trail.

.   .   .

Danny kicked a chunk of wood into the fire. Sparks flew into the air, landing in the dry duff a few feet away, smoldering. Duff was the thin matting of pine needles, decaying leaves and roots that covered the rocky ground of the northern conifer forest. A fire started at one spot could travel underneath the duff and pop up several feet away, spreading flames in all directions.

"Careful," Hank warned. "I've never seen the forest this

dry or the lakes this low." He stomped out the embers that had fallen to the ground. "When an old-growth forest like this has been protected for years from forest fires, a lot of dead wood builds up on the forest floor. All this dead wood creates tremendous fuel for a fire to burn hotter... with more destructive force... wiping out everything in its path."

"Do you think there'll be a total fire ban?" Danny was still thinking about the FIRE DANGER HIGH sign at the ranger station and the open fire time restrictions.

"If there isn't one already, there probably should be one." Hank had set the biggest pot from the cook kit, full of water, next to the fire pit as a safety measure. "We'll try to keep our fires as small as we can."

The fire grate itself was set in the ground up against a huge boulder the size of a small car tipped on its nose. The boulder seemed strangely out of place. "How do you suppose this boulder got here?" Danny was curious.

"Well, when the glaciers receded from this region they scraped this land down to bare rock. But some rocks, even big boulders like this one, were trapped inside icebergs floating on glacial lakes. When the icebergs melted the rocks were released and sunk to the bottoms of the lakes. Then the waters receded. Where we're sitting was once the bottom of a glacial lake. I'm guessing that's how this rock got here." Danny wasn't sure he believed his father's explanation, knowing how his dad liked to play tricks on him, but he decided not to question him.

"Speaking of rocks, what a great night to sleep out on the rocks under the stars." Hank looked up through the tree branches at the clear night sky speckled with sparkling diamonds. "Go get our sleeping pads and bags. I'll put out the fire." He handed Danny his flashlight.

Danny turned on the light and made his way back to the tent. He reached in through the bottom zipper of the door and quietly pulled out the two bags and pads, careful not to wake his mother and sister. By the time he got back to the fire, Hank had already poured the big pot of water onto the coals. Steam and smoke sizzled upwards. Hank set the big pot on the ground next to the fire grate.

"Come on, I'll show you something." Hank took the flashlight and led Danny out onto the wide, flat rock shelf that extended from the tree line to the water's edge, maybe seventy-five feet. They dropped their sleeping bags on the smooth gray granite. Then Hank walked to the very edge of the rock shelf, where it broke straight down into the water, like a natural dock. There, he shined the flashlight into the water. Two crayfish, wedged in between a crack in the rock, froze in the light. "Grab one!" Hank shot his hand into the water and caught one of the crayfish by its tail. The other crayfish clung to the rock. "Quick now." Hank held the light steady. Danny pushed up the sleeve of his sweatshirt and slowly moved his hand over the water. Then with a quick grab he snatched the critter out of the lake.

"I'll race you." Hank put his wiggling crayfish on the rock about four feet back from the edge. "Loser has to cook breakfast."

"You're on." Danny smiled and dropped his crayfish next to Hank's. "Go!" Both critters scrambled toward the lake, bumping into each other then apart. Danny's made it to the edge first, slipping into the dark water and disappearing into the depths. Hank's followed. "Yes! I can sleep in." Danny pumped his fist in the air.

Hank turned off his flashlight and they let their eyes adjust to the dark. A nearly full moon illuminated the lake. They laid out their rectangular foam sleeping pads, took off their shoes and crawled into their mummy bags, both looking up at the night sky.

"There's Orion's Belt, and the Big Dipper and the North Star." Danny pointed out the constellations to his father, even though he knew his father could name these constellations better than he could.

"Well I hope this year the stars are a little better aligned in our favor." Hank yawned, finally showing signs of fatigue. Danny understood that his father was referring to their bad luck on last year's trip.

"Dad," Danny wanted to ask his father before he fell asleep, "do you think I could do a solo on this trip?"

"Where'd you get that idea?"

"From Mike. He told me about his solo."

"Why do you want to do a solo?"

"I don't know... to test myself. Just one night, alone... maybe on an island. You guys could camp close by."

"I don't know, Danny. There'll be plenty of tests for you on this trip as it is."

"Will you ask Mom?"

"Okay. I won't promise you anything, but I'll talk to your mother about it. Now go to sleep." Hank fell silent, soon fast asleep.

For a long while Danny studied the stars above him, unable to fall asleep. *Could the stars really predict the future?* He wondered. *What would the stars bring them on this trip?*

Ten months earlier, in September of the year before, Danny, Mike and Hank had taken a big trip into the Quetico Provincial Park, a wilderness region like the BWCAW just across the Canadian border in northwestern Ontario. On that trip Danny had struggled mightily to keep up with his father and brother and to meet the physical challenges of the trail. But he had proven himself more than equal to the task.

On their fifth night out a violent thunderstorm ripped through their campsite. Lightning shattered a tall red pine. The upper half of the tree crashed down onto their tent, breaking both of Hank's lower legs. Mike was injured, too, but not as severely. Danny and Mike paddled for help at first light, but the weight of the rescue fell mostly on Danny's shoulders as he found the strength to carry his father's big blue wood canoe over the toughest of all Quetico portages— the Yum Yum Portage. Narrowly escaping disaster, the trip ended with floatplane evacuations of Mike and Hank to a Canadian hospital.

Lying there beneath the stars, he thought about the violent thunderstorm on Lake Kahshahpiwi that almost killed them last year—thunder, lightning, forty feet of flaming red pine landing on their tent. *Would there be another storm this year, not a thunderstorm, but a firestorm, like the one Mike had narrowly escaped in the mountains of Utah?*

The forest was dry. The lakes were low. The night was warm, unusually warm for canoe country. A southerly breeze blew in off the lake. Beneath the silver moon a lone loon cried out—its high-pitched wail drifting across the water. The eerie, haunting sound arose out of the darkness and disappeared into the night. A shiver ran up Danny's spine. He closed his eyes to the stars and fell asleep.

chapter two

WARRIOR HILL

Danny awoke with the sun. No more bad dreams had found him in the night. But an aching hip and shoulder told him he had rolled off of his sleeping pad and onto the hard rock. Cool dew had formed on top of his sleeping bag. He pulled the hood of his sweatshirt tight around his face against the morning chill. Hank was already up, rattling the cook kit and camp stove. Then Danny remembered. *Fish. I can go fishing.* He sat up and looked out over Lake Agnes. White wisps of mist rose above the water. *Perfect.* But what had he done with his fishing pole?

"What are you looking for, Dan-man?" Hank spoke quietly, watching Danny search the campsite, even looking under both canoes.

"I can't find my fishing pole."

"Didn't I warn you about the Maymaygwayshi," Hank teased. The Maymaygwayshi was an Ojibwe trickster figure, a little man like a leprechaun. Legend had it he liked to pull tricks on campers—stealing their fish, and maybe even their fishing gear. The Maymaygwayshi liked to hide in rocks along the shoreline. "Better check the rocks," Hank suggested.

Danny walked along the shoreline. "I found it," he called to his father. Funny thing, though, he could not remember leaving it where he found it. He guessed his father had hidden it, but knew he would never admit to the trick. Luckily, it was still rigged for bass. He cast a small spinner off the rock. Bam! A hard fish strike bent his pole. "I got one... on my first cast," he whispered loudly to his father. Hank joined him at the edge of the rock, net in hand. Danny played the fish back and forth, in and out with his line. In a few minutes the father-son team had landed a three-pound smallmouth bass.

"Thanks for breakfast." Hank patted Danny on the back. He unsheathed his fillet knife, and with a few quick cuts he produced two clean, boneless bass fillets. Danny took the knife and cut up the fish remains. Later he would spread them out on shoreline rocks away from the campsite as snacks for scavengers—weasels or mink, perhaps a lucky seagull.

"Go wake Maddy and Rachel." Hank motioned toward the tent. We need to get going before the wind picks up on Lac La Croix. Danny remembered last year's trip and their harrowing paddle in the wind across huge Lake Saganaga. He rinsed his hands in the water and went to wake his mother and sister.

"Romp and stomp. It's daylight on the swamp. Let's hear the pitter-patter of little feet on the forest floor." Danny uttered the camper wake-up call as he unzipped the tent door and tied back the flaps.

"No, go away," Rachel cried out.

Maddy sat up. "Come on, Rachel, it's biffy time."

"No, I hate the biffy." Rachel crawled deeper into her bag.

In the Boundary Waters Canoe Area Wilderness all campers were required to camp at U.S. Forest Service campsites with official U.S. Forest Service fire grates and official U.S. Forest Service latrines, or biffies. The biffies were fiberglass cones about two feet high with an open top the shape of a toilet seat. These cones were attached to a wooden base, and set over a hole, dug in the ground. There were no walls like an outhouse. The biffies just sat out in the forest about two hundred feet back from the fire grate, usually sheltered by some trees or bushes. But the biffy at this campsite sat in the open in the middle of a stand of red pines. It could be seen for a hundred feet from all directions, and it was even accessible to other nearby campsites. Rachel hated it.

"Well, I have to go and I'm going now." Maddy sat up and put on her running shoes. She stood up and started to head into the woods.

"Wait for me," Rachel grabbed her shoes and ran after her mother. "Do you have the towelettes?"

Meanwhile, Hank had started cooking breakfast—hashbrown potatoes and eggs, with freeze-dried orange juice, cocoa and coffee. He had cut Danny's bass fillets into four pieces, breaded them in peppered flour and dropped them into hot, sizzling oil. By the time Maddy and Rachel returned from their morning walk in the woods, breakfast was ready. Danny had set out plates and silverware on a red and white checkered tablecloth. They all sat on logs around the fire pit.

"Mmmm, did you catch this?" Maddy loved fresh-caught fish for breakfast. She put her arm around Danny's shoulder. "You can come camping with me anytime."

"Did you wash your hands after you gutted this thing?" Rachel was always worried about cleanliness. She handed the towelettes to Danny. But before he could answer her, two very tame Canada Jays dropped down right next to Rachel, pecking at her plate of potatoes. She knew her birds, and didn't move. The Gray Jays hopped closer. Then one of them grabbed a potato shred off of her plate and they both flew off. "Now I know why they're called Camp Robbers," Rachel said, "but I still don't understand why they're called Whiskey Jacks."

"I don't know either." Hank took Rachel's plate. "Why don't you help your mother with the tent and personal packs. Danny and I will wash dishes and take care of the food pack. We need to get going. I always worry about wind on Lac La Croix."

"Can I see the map? I want to see where we're going today," Rachel asked.

"After the tent and personal packs are ready, I'll show you the map."

"Do you have my Birder's Ear?"

"Yes, it's in my rucksack, but now is not the time to go listening for birds." Rachel had insisted on bringing her Birder's Ear, a sonic recording device with a small microphone dish attached to a hand-held cassette recorder. It was Rachel's plan to record various wilderness birdcalls and songs. Danny thought it was too much extra junk to bring on the trail, but Hank let her put it in his own rucksack, along with her loon whistle.

"But, listen," Rachel begged, "can't you hear the Whiskey Jacks?"

Whee-ah, chuck-chuck. Whee-ah, chuck-chuck. The birds seemed to know that Rachel was their friend.

"No, bird-girl, we gotta' get going before the wind comes up on Lac La Croix."

"Ohhh!" Rachel stomped her foot.

"Come on, Rachel." Maddy led the way back to the tent.

It took them another hour to pack up. Hank and Danny set the food pack and cook kit by water's edge on the rock ledge, along with Hank's rucksack. Hank had packed their trail lunch, or TL, for the day in a nylon bag. He had placed the high energy snack inside the very top of the food pack, along with the sierra cups and a fresh bottle of bug juice. Maddy and Rachel followed with the two personal packs and the tent.

"Come on, Rachel." Danny led his little sister back to the fire pit. He showed her how he had cleaned out the ashes and left a stack of split firewood. He had even set up a teepee fire in the fire grate, all ready for the next campers to light. "Remember our family motto," he said earnestly to Rachel, "Foresters leave no trace." He handed her a stick of firewood.

"Okay," said Rachel. "Foresters leave no trace." They threw their sticks down on the firewood pile and ran over to their parents waiting to load the canoes.

Canoeing as a Forester also meant wet-boot camping with wood-and-canvas canoes. The family owned three such canoes: an eighteen-foot White Otter, painted navy blue; a seventeen-foot Old Town, painted forest green; and a seven-teen-foot Seliga, red, built by the famous canoe builder named Joe Seliga, who lived in Ely. For this trip, the Foresters would take the green Old Town and the red Seliga. These

were beautiful, handcrafted cedar canoes, covered with canvas skins, sealed and painted. They handled wonderfully in
the water, but could not be run up on the rocks. So the
Foresters wet-boot camped. At the beginning and end of
every portage, or at campsite landings, they stepped knee-
deep into the water to load and unload the canoes, rather
than dragging the canoes up on the rocks, which might tear
the canvas bellies. This was the Forester way of camping—
their way and their tradition.

Before loading the wood canoes, Hank spread the map for
the day out on the flat rock surface. "Rachel, see where we
came from yesterday." He drew his finger along the Moose
River to their Lake Agnes campsite. "Today we go here." He
drew his finger into the narrows at the north end of Lake
Agnes, across two portages, and onto Lac La Croix, a huge
lake that straddled the U.S./Canadian border and defined the
western boundary of the BWCAW. He pointed to more features on the map. "There's Warrior Hill, there're the pictographs and there's where we hope to camp tonight." He
folded the map into a clear plastic map case to carry with
him in the canoe. A compass was attached to the map with a
lanyard. "Let's go, campers!" It would be their second day on
the trail.

The sun had already climbed high above the trees, hot
again in the cloudless sky. Once the packs were loaded into
the canoes, Danny paddled bow in the green Old Town, with
Maddy in the stern seat. Hank and Rachel took the red Seliga.
Rachel always sat in front. Maddy, fair-skinned and blonde,
wore green cotton hospital scrubs and a broad-brimmed gar-
dener's hat. She applied sunscreen to her bare arms, neck and
face. Rachel wore her big-pocket khaki shorts, a white T-shirt
and a pith helmet with mosquito netting rolled up around
the brim. She looked more like a jungle explorer than a
northwoods camper. Her yellow waterproof camera hung on

a red lanyard around her neck. Like her father, jet black hair, she tanned without ever burning. Hank and Danny were already in their swimsuits, anticipating another hot day. But true to the Forester tradition, they all wore their boots and life jackets.

Paddling north out of Lake Agnes, they entered the Boulder River, soon walking the canoes down a shallow set of rapids. Hank led the way, with Rachel still riding in the bow. Twice he bent over to clear the narrow channel of sharp rocks for safe passage. Danny and his mother followed. The first portage lay just ahead, a rocky path twenty-four rods in length. The experienced campers made quick work of it, carrying their packs and canoes along the trail.

After crossing a wide bend in the river they were met by a group of four men, unshaven and rough looking, coming the other way just off the portage to Lac La Croix. They were paddling aluminum canoes loaded with mountains of fishing gear. Hank referred to aluminum canoes as "'lumies." They passed the group with only a curt "good morning," nothing more. Then they landed at the portage, a sixty-five rod trail through the woods, uphill, then down to the lake.

"How long is a rod again?" Rachel asked her father.

"Sixteen and a half feet."

"Why do they use rods to measure portages? Whoever heard of rods? Why not yards, or meters like in Canada?"

"I don't know. I guess rods is just the traditional English measurement for portages." Danny could tell his father was already bracing himself for Rachel's daily barrage of questions about the world around her.

Hank put the lightest personal pack, a #2 Duluth pack, on Rachel's back. She also carried the cook kit. Then he pulled on his own rucksack and flipped the Seliga up onto his shoulders in one smooth movement. "Stay with me now," he instructed Rachel. Maddy would carry the Old Town. She and

Danny had mastered the two-person canoe flip. She, too, took off with a spring in her step, leaving the food pack and second personal for Danny to double-pack. He had learned the pack flip and double-packing method from Mike on last summer's trip. Loaded front and back, including the tent, he followed his mother. Fifteen minutes later, he was standing on the steep trail, looking out over magnificent Lac La Croix.

Hank had already walked into the water and flipped his canoe down. He grabbed Rachel's pack off her back and set it in the stern, along with the cook kit. Maddy walked into the water and flipped down, too, her canoe landing with a splash. She let out a groan of relief and rubbed her shoulders, waiting by the Old Town for Danny.

"There it is." Hank scanned Boulder Bay, the very southeastern end of the lake. The whole of the Lac La Croix could not be seen from any one view. It stretched for more than twenty miles, first north, then spreading out to the west—a vast complex of deep bays and big islands, with plenty of open water—big water. It even had its own smell—a big lake smell.

"Wow!" Maddy exclaimed. "I forgot how much I love this lake. I bet it's been twenty years since I've paddled Lac La Croix."

Danny recognized the scent of the big lake. After all, he had paddled Saganaga and Kawnipi and Kahshahpiwi with his father and brother. But it was not an especially comforting smell. He remembered the wind and waves on big Sag and the storm on Kahshahpiwi that had almost killed them last summer.

"Danny, it's your turn to paddle stern." If his mother sensed his fear, she didn't let on. She was offering him the stern on the big lake as if she had full confidence in his paddling ability.

"Okay." Danny held the boat steady while Maddy

climbed into the bow.

"Parts of Lac La Croix are stream-fed and other parts are spring fed." Hank talked as they paddled away from shore. "Some parts are shallow and other parts are very deep. So there are whole different fish habitats and whole different ecosystems all over this lake, yet it's all one whole, like a living organism."

"What about the birds?" Rachel wanted to know.

"The same," Hank answered, "all kinds of different birds, even pelicans and cormorants."

Danny could feel the wind at their backs. He paddled hard and steady, using mostly his J-stroke to steer, but an occasional C-stroke. It would still require another mile of paddling north before their first sighting of Warrior Hill. Then, rounding a point, he caught a glimpse of the rock face.

Warrior Hill stood out against the darkly forested landscape like the white head of a bald eagle against a dark green jack pine. Rising nearly two hundred feet out of the water, the wide, smooth slope of gray granite could be spotted a mile away. At first, to Danny, it didn't seem that impressive, not quite what he had expected; but as they approached from the south the hill grew and grew in size until he realized the enormity of the rock feature. He tried to imagine himself as a young warrior, swimming across the lake, then running up the steep rock slope to claim his place in the tribe. *Not possible, not for me,* he thought. *Maybe for Mike—he's the family warrior.* He remembered the fierceness of Mike's anger, driving away in his truck.

As they crossed the open water, Danny shouted over to Rachel in the green canoe, "Watch for the underwater chain, now. It's painted red and white, running right along the border, just up ahead. I think I see it!"

"I'm not falling for that stupid trick." Rachel sneered at her brother. "There's no red and white border chain between

Canada and America."

Danny looked at his father, who just shrugged his shoulders. He wouldn't go along with the joke. *How come I'm always the one people play tricks on in this family, and never Rachel?* Danny thought to himself, remembering the trip with his father and brother, and their tricking him about the underwater border chain.

They were approaching Warrior Hill. Up close the shoreline presented a barrier of sharp boulders exposed in the low water—teeth-like rocks that would surely tear open the bottom of either wood canoe. The wind picked up. Simultaneously both Hank and Danny turned left, steering their vessels east to west across the base of Warrior Hill. Rachel snapped photos with her waterproof camera, aiming upward from her seat in the red canoe.

"There's no place to land," Hank called over to Maddy.

"The beach. There's a beach around the point." She pointed to the western edge of the rock formation. Danny was always amazed by his parents' memories for features of the land in canoe country, as if the time they had spent here twenty-five years ago had etched indelible memories into their minds.

Ten minutes later they were unloading the canoes on a sand and gravel beach in a small shallow cove just to the west of Warrior Hill. Small waves washed rhythmically over the pebbles along the shore. Hank and Danny two-manned both canoes out of the water, setting them in the sand. "We're in Canada, now," Hank announced. "Warrior Hill is in the Quetico." He seemed proud to claim the landmark for his own country—Canada—where he had been born and raised.

Maddy pulled the trail lunch bag out of the food pack, along with a bottle of bug juice. "Come on," she waved, and energetically led them up a steep path. Rachel followed her mother. Hank, though, put on his rucksack and limped over to where the edge of the beach met the slope of Warrior Hill. There, at water's edge, he lifted up a boulder about the size of a bowling ball and started to carry it with him up the trail to the top of the little mountain.

"What're you doing, Dad?" Danny asked.

"I'll tell you when we get to the top," Hank laughed. "Get a rock yourself if you want to."

Danny ran over to the same spot his father had picked up the bowling ball boulder. He found one just like it, but a little smaller, and lifted it up, carrying it next to his stomach as he walked. *What's my dad up to, now?* he wondered; but he followed him anyway, like he always did. Then he remembered his father telling him stories about rolling boulders down the face of Warrior Hill. *That must be it—boulder rolling!*

They made it to the top, Hank and Danny huffing and puffing, dropping their boulders, laughing at their own stupidity, and falling down on the ground. What idiots would carry boulders to the top of Warrior Hill? Maddy and Rachel shook their heads. They had stopped ten yards short of the edge of the slope, in the shelter of a mountain maple bush, out of the wind.

"What on earth are you two doing?" Maddy stood with her hands on her hips.

"I'll tell you after we eat. I promise." Hank smiled wryly.

Maddy broke open the TL pack. Rachel set out the sierra cups and gave the bottle of bug juice a shake. Together they portioned out the trail lunch—three crackers, a cube of cheese, a chunk of salami, a handful of gorp and a twist of red licorice for each person. Maddy set out a container of peanut butter. Together, then, each with cup in hand, the four Foresters walked to the very top edge of Warrior Hill, wind blowing in their hair, the hot sun climbing higher and higher. And there, overlooking vast Lac La Croix, the laughter was replaced with awe.

"Gee," Rachel broke the silence. "I can see where we came from this morning. And look at those guys—they look tiny from up here." Rachel pointed to a group of canoeists paddling across a distant bay to the west.

"Check that out." Hank pointed even farther west to the horizon above the tree line where gray-white smoke boiled up into the sky, moving south to north. "That must be the Crane Lake fire we heard about on the news. Let's hope this wind doesn't switch to the west, or good-bye BWCAW."

"Why don't we all sit down," Maddy suggested.

Hank sat cross-legged and dug his binoculars and Rachel's listening dish out of his small pack. He handed the device to Rachel. "See what you can pick up from that direction." He pointed again to the west. Then he adjusted his binoculars.

"Shish, I hear a plane engine." Rachel carefully aimed the Birder's Ear with her right hand and pressed the earphone hard against her left ear.

"There!" Danny almost shouted. "I see two planes—a bigger one and a smaller one."

"I got 'em." Hank talked as he watched. "The Canadians must be helping out the Americans. The big plane is a Canadair CL-215... amphibious. Only the Canadians use those. They can scoop up fourteen hundred gallons of water to drop on the fire. The smaller plane is American... a Forest Service Dehavilland Beaver." He handed his binoculars to Danny. "The news said four thousand acres, and it still wasn't under control. That was two days ago. Looks like a bigger fire now."

"Look! I can see the big one dropping water!" Danny followed the path of the plane.

"Let me see." Rachel reached up. Danny pulled her to her feet and helped her focus the binoculars. Hank stood up, too. For a while they all stood together, watching the smoke. Then Maddy spoke up.

"Let's finish eating, guys." She would keep them on task.

So they sat together in the hot summer wind atop Warrior Hill, eating their trail lunch, passing a bottle of grape-flavored bug juice, looking out over the lake.

"How far did the warriors have to swim before they reached the bottom of the hill?" Rachel asked.

"No one really knows," Maddy answered.

"Do you think they started way over there on shore, or jumped in the water from a canoe in the middle of the lake?"

"I never really thought about that," Maddy answered again.

"Did they do it in the daytime or at night, because I was kind of imagining the warriors had to run up the hill between two lines of torches? That would really be cool."

"Rachel, it's a legend. What we know is all we know. I don't know the answers to all your questions." Maddy tried to steer her off the subject.

"Then answer one thing you do know," Rachel insisted.

"Okay, I'll try."

"Is Mike in that fire?" She started to cry. "I don't want Mike to get burned again. I love Mike." She cried even louder, sobbing.

Maddy took her in her arms and looked up at Hank. He knelt beside them and put his hand on Rachel's shoulder. "Mike's going to be just fine, little one. He's as tough as any young man who ever climbed Warrior Hill; and I know he'd be very happy to see you standing here right now, looking out over Lac La Croix. I remember one of Mike's first trips with me. He was about your age. It was in late August. We left the big blue canoe and the packs down at the beach and carried our sleeping bags up here. That night we slept under the stars and watched the Northern Lights. That's why this is Mike's very favorite spot in all of the Boundary Waters and Quetico."

Danny remembered Mike once telling him that if he ever died he wanted to be cremated and have his ashes scattered on top of Warrior Hill. He guessed that now was not a good time to tell this to Rachel, or his parents. But if he were to give his answer to Rachel's question—he knew for certain that Mike was on the front lines of that fire.

"Come on, Rachel, we have to get going." Maddy took her hand.

"Don't forget the boulders." Hank jumped up. He and Danny ran for their rocks and carried them to the top of the hill. Danny was ready to roll his boulder and watch it splash into Lac La Croix, but his father stopped to make a speech. "In the old days we would camp with cans and bottles, and sink them in the middle of the lake, but we no longer do this. And we used to wash our dishes and bathe with soap in the lake, but we no longer do this. And we used to roll boulders down the face of Warrior Hill, but this was not wise either. So to make amends for all the boulders I have rolled down Warrior Hill, we carried these two replacement rocks up here." He grinned at Danny and dropped his rock on the ground.

Danny shook his head. He thought he was going to be able to boulder roll, like in the old days. But his father had tricked him, like a Maymaygwayshi. He considered for a moment rolling his rock down the hill anyway, but he dropped it hard on the ground, too. "I'll get you. You wait and see. Before this trip is over, Maymaygwayshi will strike." He smiled and pointed his finger at his dad, then turned and ran down the path to the beach.

Down below, at lake level, the wind had picked up. Bigger waves were washing farther up onto the gravel. Hank lifted Rachel into the bow of the Seliga, took the stern for himself and shoved off into the wind and waves. Danny set his paddle in the back of the Old Town, but his mother brushed him aside. "I'll take the stern, now." She held the boat steady for Danny to step into the bow, then she, too, shoved off. Danny understood that in the stronger wind and waves his mother wanted control from the stern. She may not have been as physically powerful as his father, but she could handle a canoe as well as him any day.

They paddled just a short distance into the wind, rounded a small point and headed north again with the wind and sun at their backs. Lac La Croix lay before them like a vast maze. This lake scared Danny. Even on the map Lac La Croix seemed too big, too complex for his strength and skill. He preferred the smaller lakes, like Agnes. They felt easier, safer. For all its beauty, Lac La Croix was a hungry wolf of a lake— Danny could sense this. A shiver ran up his spine.

"What was that?" Maddy had caught his shiver.

"I don't know," said Danny. "I just got a funny feeling about this lake."

"I know what you mean." His mother reassured him. "You'll be okay with me in the stern." Danny nodded his head, indicating that he had heard his mother. Just then they sighted a series of shear cliffs to the east. Hank and Rachel led the way, angling across the waves of a wide bay. Before long they reached the site of the ancient rock art.

The pictograph cliffs, rust-colored, pink, gray-green stone, stood like a fortress wall, a hundred feet high, over-hanging the water. On a rock ledge, sixty feet above the paddlers, a pair of bald eagles had built a huge nest, but no eaglets were in sight. On the cliff face below the overhanging rock, about eight feet above the water line, the Foresters found the Native American rock paintings, untouched for centuries.

"I see a moose!" Rachel called back to Danny. "Two moose!"

As Danny and his mother caught up to his sister and his father, the rust-colored pictographs revealed themselves. They found a multitude of handprints, the full profile of a bull moose and the front half of another bull moose. Not far from the two moose images stood a stick figure of a human holding a spear or bow and arrow. All of the rock paintings were no bigger than a handprint.

"They're estimated to be three to four hundred years old," Hank lectured in his art instructor's voice. Both canoes bobbed in the waves—no good place to land. "I always try to imagine who painted them, and why."

"What did they use for paint?" It was Rachel again with more of her questions.

"No one really knows, Rachel. We think they used a crushed iron rock called hematite, mixed with a glue made from sturgeon cartilage or mixed with fish oil or bear fat. As the animal fat decomposed and disappeared, the hematite chemically attached to the rock face of the cliffs. That's why the pictographs are reddish-colored. They're very fragile, so we shouldn't touch them."

"Did they paint them standing in canoes in the summer, or did they stand on the ice in the winter?"

"That's another thing no one really knows," Hank answered. "I always wonder what the water levels of the lakes were back then."

"I always get a strange feeling here," Maddy talked quietly, as if in church. "I just know these are some kind of ceremonial waters. The First Peoples had religion and art and stories just like we do. These may be pictures of the sacred dreams of ancient tribal healers—medicine men or women. We should be very respectful of this place."

Danny thought about his mother's words as they sat silently studying the pictographs. *What kind of ceremonies and dreams was she talking about?* he wondered, but didn't want to break the silence to ask. He remembered again his Mike-on-fire dream.

Rachel snapped some more pictures before Hank turned their canoe away from the cliffs. Maddy turned, too. All four Foresters hit their paddle strokes simultaneously, keeping a rhythm. They headed north again, angling east-to-west back across a wide expanse of Lac La Croix. The waves had grown even bigger in the midday wind. Whitecaps nipped the air ahead of them. Again, Danny sensed the restless power of the lake.

For another two miles or more they tracked north, paddling in unison, pushed along by the wind at their backs, the sun high in the sky. Maddy tied her hat down. Slowly they made their way to where the jagged western shoreline opened up into Fish Stake Narrows. There, they turned due west. Hank scanned the map. He pulled in next to a low cliff along the south shoreline of the narrows, out of the wind. Maddy followed, maneuvering the Old Town alongside the Seliga. Hank and Maddy studied the map from their side-by-side stern seats. Danny and Rachel rested their paddles across the bow gunwales. It was the first anyone had spoken since leaving the pictographs.

"Where are we?" Maddy asked.

"Here," Hank pointed to a spot on the map, "and we want to get to here for tonight." He showed Maddy the route. "I call it Wounded Paw Peninsula because it reminds me of a mangled bear paw. Not everyone can see the campsite from the lake, so it still might be available." They had spotted other campers on the lake—campers who had already claimed campsites for the night. They knew they would have to find a campsite before too long, or end up pushing on later and later to find one.

"I'm tired," Rachel complained. "This route is too long." She hung her head in the bow.

"Don't give up, camper. It's not much farther, just a couple of miles straight ahead." Hank pushed away from the low cliff and paddled with a surprising burst of power. "Just lily-dip if you have to, but don't quit on me." Whirlpools spun in the water off the end of his paddle blade. Danny and his mother hustled to catch up. Hank could still show his great canoeing strength when he wanted to.

To the west, then, they paddled hard, hiding in the lee of the south shoreline to stay out of the wind. Hank and Rachel led by the length of three canoes until a half-hour later when they ran out of protective shoreline and entered the open top of Lady Boot Bay—wide open waters with no shelter from the wind. There the waves hit hard, slapping the Seliga broadside. Rachel dropped her paddle in the bow and grabbed both gunwales to steady herself. Hank turned his head, calling back just one word from the stern. "Missepishu!" Danny heard his father shout the name of the mythical Ojibwe water panther.

Then Hank pointed to a rocky peninsula just ahead.

Danny and his mother followed. Minutes later they were unloading their canoe in the shallow waters of Wounded Paw Peninsula—a stubby hook of rock that crooked back on itself, creating a small hidden cove wedged up against the mainland. The floor of the cove was shallow, all pebbles and gravel, perfect for landing the wood canoes. Only a few boulders rested along the shoreline. And most conveniently, a wide swath of smooth granite sloped gradually up to the campsite, allowing for an easy haul of canoes and gear.

Rachel ran up into the campsite. "It's perfect!" she shouted back to her family. "Someone even left a pile of split firewood... and we don't have to share the biffy."

Hank flipped up the Seliga and started up the rock slope, his wounded legs wobbling a bit unsteadily. Danny lifted the stern of the Old Town, Maddy the bow. Together they carried the green canoe behind Hank. When he flipped down, they set the Old Town down, too, upside down, resting close to the Seliga.

Up in the campsite Danny understood their good luck, or perhaps his father's good judgment in leading them to this place. Here they had found a fantastic Boundary Waters campsite with a spectacular view of the lake. Huge red pines, maybe three hundred years old, stood as far back into the mainland as Danny could see—a stand of trees that had never been logged. The forest floor was nearly level and carpeted with a thick mat of dry pine needles. There was room enough for twenty tents.

"Let's go swimming!" Rachel hopped up and down.

"Okay, okay, but first let's set up the tent." Maddy grabbed Rachel by the hand to go fetch the tent. Hank and Danny would be left to carry the packs up into the campsite.

In twenty minutes, Maddy and Rachel had the tent pitched. They had laid out everyone's sleeping bags and were changing into their swimming suits inside the tent. Rachel giggled with excitement. In the meantime, Hank and Danny had set up the kitchen area. They spread out a blue nylon tarp, held down with a big rock on each corner. Danny built a fire for them to light later. Hank strung a nylon mesh hammock between two reddish tree trunks back and away from the fire pit, a great place to nap. But for now, in the late afternoon heat, they would all go swimming in the cool waters of beautiful Lac La Croix.

The thought of swimming reminded Danny of his junior high school. Swimming for gym class was one of his least favorite things to do. He was not a strong swimmer and always took to the end of the line for any swimming tests. At the end of the school year, he barely passed the Junior Lifesaving course. Secretly, he hoped he'd never be called upon to actually rescue someone.

"Hurry up!" Rachel called.

The Forester swim-with-boots-on rule would still apply as a precaution against cut feet. But in the shallow waters of the cove, Maddy and Hank allowed the life jackets, or PFDs, to be left on shore. So in their boots and swimsuits, towels around their necks, they clomped back down to the lake.

Maddy reapplied her sunscreen. "I can't be out here too long."

Hank limped stiffly behind them. "I'm glad we're off the lake." He pointed northwest, out past where the cove opened up onto the big water—whitecaps everywhere. "That's not even the widest part of this lake."

Danny looked to where his father was pointing. "Missepishu," he said out loud.

"Yes, Missepishu," Hank answered.

"Forget Missepishu. Let's go swimming." Rachel laughed and jumped into the water.

Maddy followed, then Hank, and Danny last. Like a family

of river otters, they frolicked and floated in the late afternoon sun until they felt completely cooled and cleaned and had tired of the fun.

"Time to fix dinner." Maddy stood up in a shallow spot. Then she froze in her place. "Listen!" she whispered loudly.

"Help!" The cry came in across the water, fighting against the wind.

"Shish! Did you hear that?"

"Hear what?" Hank asked.

"Be quiet," Maddy whispered again. Everyone listened.

"Help!" Another long cry came in off the lake, caught in the curve of the cove like Rachel's listening dish.

"I heard that." Hank stood up, cupped his hands behind his ears and turned toward the open lake.

"Help!" This time the cry was unmistakably a woman's voice.

Hank, the tallest, scanned the rough waters, sun reflecting off the waves. "There!" He pointed. Out on the lake, perhaps a quarter of a mile away, a lone canoe floundered broadside in the waves. One of the occupants was waving a paddle in the air and screaming for help. "Maddy?" Hank called out, asking for her leadership.

"Follow me," she said calmly. "Just follow me."

chapter three

SWAMPED

Maddy was first to scramble out of the water, up the rocks and into the campsite. She headed straight for the first aid kit. Hank followed, lifting Rachel in his arms. "Danny, get the paddles and life jackets!" he hollered over his shoulder. Danny paused for just a moment, listening again, intently, then he ran for the paddles.

Up in the campsite Hank pulled his binoculars out of his rucksack. Turning toward the lake he focused the lenses. "I can see three people with packs in a 'lumi. It looks like the guy in the stern is hurting somehow. He's down on his knees, arms across his chest. I can't see his paddle. Looks like a woman in the bow and someone in the duffer seat are turning around." Danny and Rachel stood beside their father, peering out over the lake as he narrated the scene more and more excitedly. "No one's paddling! The wind's got 'em turned broadside against the waves! Oh-man! They are definitely in some kind of trouble! Oh-oh! Oh-no! They just swamped!"

"Dr. Madeline," Hank yelled, "it's decision time!" Maddy lifted her head up from the first aid kit and looked out over the angry lake where the swamped campers bobbed helplessly between the whitecaps. "Code Red!" Hank yelled. She joined the threesome by the fire pit, wearing her stethoscope around her neck. She had already zipped up her life jacket, pockets stuffed with first aid supplies in plastic bags, including a plastic airway for CPR.

Who goes and who stays?—was the first question on Danny's mind. *Where's Mike when we need him?*—was the second. Hank looked at Maddy and Maddy looked at Hank. Danny had the idea that his parents had been through this before and knew what to do without even speaking. They nodded knowingly to each other. Then Maddy turned to her daughter. "Rachel, I do not like leaving you alone in this campsite, but we are going to need three pairs of hands out there. We need Danny with us. Promise me you will stay put. Please, sit on this log and do not move. "

"I promise, Mom," Rachel said seriously. "I'll sit right here." She sat down on a fat fire pit log and faced the lake. Maddy threw a towel over her wet shoulders and gave her a quick hug. Hank handed her his binoculars. "You can watch us the whole time. We'll be right back, sweetheart."

"The Seliga… it'll be more stable in the waves." Hank motioned to Danny and quickly they two-manned the red canoe into the lake. Maddy was already standing knee deep in the clear water, paddle in hand. Hank threw a length of rope into the stern compartment. Danny started to step into the bow.

"No-no," his mother put her hand on his shoulder. "Get in the middle." Danny looked at his father.

"She said get in the middle!" Hank pointed to the duffer's spot, irritated that Danny would question his mother's judgment at a time like this.

Danny knew they were right—the expert paddlers, the old camp team, Hank in the stern and Maddy in the bow—they would know exactly what to do out there in the big waves. He tightened his PFD and climbed into the duffer's seat, facing Maddy, his back against the yoke.

Hank held the boat steady for his paddling partner, then pushed off from the stern. "Let's go!" he shouted. "Lemme' know if you want to switch sides." Maddy nodded her head without looking back. Together they hit their powerful, even strokes into the water as they paddled out and away from the protection of the sheltered bay—out from safety and into danger—with Danny along for the ride.

"Are we going to try a sea rescue?" Danny shouted in the wind. He had learned about a sea rescue from Mike. It was when the rescue canoeists pulled the swamped canoe out of the water upside down across the rescue canoe's gunwales, then turned the swamped canoe right side up, empty of water, and pushed it back into the lake so the swamped campers could climb back into it. In theory it could work, but in big waves...?

"No!" he heard Hank shout, "too dangerous." It was the answer he had expected.

Out on the open lake the hot wind and heavy waves caught them from behind, fish-tailing the keel as Hank steered north. At water level, in the big waves, they couldn't see the swamped campers. Danny knew his father must have lined up a spot on the horizon, probably a tall white pine, with his last sighting of the aluminum canoe. Still, they would need plenty of luck to find them. "I wonder who those guys are?" Danny said, more thinking out loud than asking a question.

"Idiots!" came the answer from his father.

"Switch on three," Maddy called out. " One... two... three..." and the paddlers switched sides, pulling hard against the water to stay ahead of the push of the waves. Then came a loud whooshing sound as the biggest whitecap yet broke over the stern, dumping water into the canoe. *Missepishu*, Danny thought to himself, *the water panther—wildly thrashing its tail.*

"Bail!" Hank yelled. Danny grabbed a big sponge tied to a rope and began sopping up the water and squeezing it out over the side of the canoe. He had done this before, on big Lake Saganaga a year ago with his father and Mike. He never thought he'd be bailing on this trip.

"There!" Maddy pointed her paddle out to the left of the bow. Someone was waving a paddle in the air, barely visible above the waves, maybe forty yards ahead of them. Whoosh! Another wave broke over the stern. For such a hot day, the water felt icy cold to Danny. He concentrated on bailing as the lake became their whole world—a wild and frightening world inhabited by a wild mythical beast, Missepishu, wanting to swallow them up. Dry land already seemed a long ways behind them.

"When we get up there, I'll keep the canoe steady in the waves. Danny, you may have to get in the water to help. Maddy's in charge of first aid." Hank's loud orders blew past with the wind. "I can see them! There!"

"Look out!" Maddy screamed.

"Whoa! Hang on!" Hank yelled.

Without warning another great wave swept the Foresters' canoe right on top and across the center of the overturned aluminum canoe, making a loud screeching sound as wood scraped against metal. They splashed down on the other side. The two canoes formed a big T in the water—the swamped canoe lying east-west, the Foresters sitting north-south. A man, a woman and a teenaged girl clung to one end of the silver canoe.

"Help us!" the woman cried out. "I think my husband's had a heart attack." She held one arm onto their canoe and one arm tight around the man's neck, keeping his head just above water. His face looked clammy white, like the wet belly of a fish. His lips had turned blue. His eyes were open, but he wasn't talking. Bigger and bigger waves broke over the belly of the aluminum canoe.

"Hold steady, folks, I'm a doctor, an E.R. doctor," Maddy tried to reassure them. "We're going to get you out of here, but first I need a look at him." Hank back-paddled, keeping their canoe perpendicular to the waves while Maddy talked. "What's his name?"

"Bill."

"What's your name?"

"Anne Tucker, and this is our daughter, Julie." A girl

maybe Danny's age, maybe older, with blond hair and a scratched, sunburned face, clung to the canoe behind her mother and father. They all wore life jackets. Danny could see that the girl was frightened.

"Okay, listen carefully and follow my every instruction." Maddy took charge of the situation. "Bill, can you hear me?" Bill weakly raised his hand out of the water. "Good. Now first we're going to pull Bill into our canoe. Then I want you two to get back in your canoe, full of water, and paddle while we tow you back to shore. Got that?" Mother and daughter nodded their heads. By now Maddy had turned around backwards in the bow seat, facing Hank and Danny.

"Hurry up, Maddy," Hank spoke between clenched teeth. They had just taken on another wave. Danny kept up his bailing. "Get him over here!" Hank shouted at Anne to swim her husband next to the Seliga. But she couldn't seem to move, didn't seem to know what to do. "Danny, go get him."

Danny looked at Maddy. "You can do it." She gave him her confident mother look. *Man, I'm not that good of a swimmer,* Danny thought to himself, but with his heart pounding and adrenaline pumping he jumped into the water.

It was worse than he had imagined—trying to swim in the big waves. He swallowed a mouthful of lake and sputtered, thankful for his PFD. Quickly, though, he made his way to the half-drowned man and his panicked wife. "I got him," he said to Anne, grabbing the back of Bill's life jacket.

Whoosh! Another great wave broke over the 'lumi, washing Bill, Anne and Danny right next to Hank in the stern of the wood canoe. Now Maddy paddled to keep the Seliga squared against the waves. Hank grabbed Bill by the back of his shirt. "Danny, get around to the other side and hold steady on the gunwale to counterbalance when I pull him into the canoe— on three!" Hank was still shouting in the wind.

Danny hesitated.

"Now!" his father ordered, pointing downwards.

Danny took a deep breath and ducked under the belly of the canoe, hoping the lake wouldn't swallow him up. But he popped up on the other side and grabbed the gunwale with both hands near the yoke.

"Good man!" Hank yelled. "Ready... one... two..."

Then suddenly, unexpectedly, the girl, Julie, let go of the swamped canoe and grabbed onto the Forester's canoe opposite Danny. Her white fingers gripped the wooden gunwale, pulling it down, tipping the whole boat. Whoosh! Another giant wave hit hard. Water poured in over the side.

"No!" Hank yelled angrily. And with a hard swing of his paddle he brought the wooden blade down with a crack on the girl's fingers.

"Ouch!" She let go, sinking back into the water.

"Hank!" Maddy screamed, face red with anger.

"Maddy!" Hank yelled back. "She was gonna' swamp us." Then he turned to the man in the water. "Danny," he called over his shoulder, "on three... one... two... three!" With a loud growl and his bear-like strength, Hank Forester pulled Bill Tucker out of the panther's mouth and into the stern of his red canoe. Bill was a big man, heavy. He clutched his chest, shivering.

"Talk to me Bill. Where does it hurt?" Maddy reached out for his head and shoulders as Hank laid him on his back and slid him along the bottom of the canoe toward the doctor. "Any history of heart problems? Any medications?" She felt his neck for a pulse, then pulled out her stethoscope and listened as best she could to his chest.

But now even bigger waves came at them from the south. Hank strained with the blade of his new paddle to keep them steady in the water. "You and you." Hank pointed to the women in the water. "Get back to your canoe, turn it over and get into it. Danny! You paddle stern with them." Danny ducked under the Seliga again, bobbing up beside the women. Hank threw him his paddle.

"Come on, I'll show you." Danny's parents had taught him this swamped canoe paddling method. In the rolling waves they turned the canoe upright. It was an outfitter's canoe with a logo painted on the bow. Underneath, luckily, they found two paddles floating, but only one pack. Danny guessed it was their personal pack—sleeping bags and clothing—stuff that would float for a while in a plastic pack liner. "Where's your food pack and tent?" he asked the mother.

"Bottom of the lake," she answered. Then she turned toward Maddy and shouted above the wind and waves, "How's my husband?"

Maddy had propped Bill's head and shoulders up with Rachel's life jacket. "He's breathing. He can talk. I think it is his heart. I gave him some aspirin. All we can do is get him back to land, then I can do more."

"Maddy, here." Hank tossed her the rope. "We don't dare turn around in these waves." So they would paddle the canoe backwards—Maddy paddling stern kneeling backwards in front of the bow seat, and Hank paddling bow kneeling backwards in front of the stern seat. Maddy tied one end of the rope to the bow seat and threw the other end to Danny in the water. He tied it to the front of the aluminum canoe.

"Get in," he told the women. "Paddle as best you can, all three of us. Even though it's full of water, it'll still move." He had strapped their pack to the bow thwart. Mother knelt in the bow. Daughter knelt right behind the yoke. Danny took the stern.

"Okay!" Hank yelled. Together he and Maddy dug their paddles into the turbulent water—big wave after big wave coming at them from the south, whitecaps all around. Slowly, ever so slowly, they turned the submerged canoe with its three paddlers into the wind with them, towing them behind.

As they turned, it was the first chance Danny had to look back at the campsite. He guessed that from the time they had stopped they had drifted another hundred yards north. Facing into the wind and paddling a swamped canoe felt like swimming in wet cement. Below the surface of the water they had to brace their legs to hold onto the canoe. Above the surface, paddling was all arms—exhausting. All the while wave after wave washed over them.

"Good job!" Danny shouted encouragement to mother and daughter, though he wasn't sure he believed his own words. "We're gonna' make it!" It was then that he first noticed the girl's left hand on the grip of her paddle, attached with some kind of a special strap. It was an artificial hand—a prosthetic hand and forearm extending from her elbow. He thought about his father cracking her fingers with his paddle, and felt a twinge of embarrassment. *How can she paddle that well,* he thought to himself, *with one artificial hand and one bruised hand?*

Up in front of them he could see his parents straining hard with each stroke. The sun angled off the west. It would take them nearly an hour, struggling all the way, to make it back to shore. When they reached the shelter of the cove, Maddy cut the towrope with her Swiss army knife. She and Hank surged ahead with her E.R. patient. When they reached the shoreline, Danny could see Hank lift Bill out of the canoe and carry him over his shoulders, like a firefighter, up and into the campsite. Rachel was there, at water's edge, with the first aid kit.

When Danny and Anne and Julie Tucker finally reached the shallows, the two women waded to shore, then half-ran, half-crawled up and into the campsite. Danny abandoned the canoe and wrestled their waterlogged pack up onto the rocks, just out of the lake. Waterlogged himself, he collapsed onto the pack, exhausted, feeling sick to his stomach from the lake water he had swallowed. He let the swamped 'lumi slosh in the waves—something he never would have done with a wood canoe.

By the time he made his way up into the campsite, Hank and Maddy had found dry clothes for Bill—a pair of Hank's sweatpants and a T-shirt. They had propped him up on a sleeping pad at the base of a huge, fire-scarred red pine to elevate his head and chest. Some of the color had returned to his face, and his lips no longer looked blue. His wife and daughter knelt beside him.

"He may have had a heart attack," Maddy explained, "but he seems to have stabilized. I've given him some medication in addition to the aspirin. For now, all we can do is monitor his symptoms and have him rest."

Bill looked up at Maddy, sunburn showing on his bald head. "Thank you," he whispered, "and you and you and you." He pointed weakly to Hank, then Danny, then Rachel.

Anne Tucker held his right hand. "What do we do now?" she asked.

"We S-T-O-P," said Maddy, "Stay-Think-Organize-Plan. We're not going anywhere tonight, not on this lake. So first things first, let's get you two into some dry clothes. Then we'll talk about what to do tomorrow." Maddy led the women toward the Forester's tent. As they walked, Maddy called back over her shoulder to Hank and Danny. "This is girl stuff. You boys go fetch some firewood." Danny sensed that his mother was still angry with his father for cracking Julie Tucker on her knuckles with his paddle.

"Follow me." Hank handed Danny a dry T-shirt. They were both still wearing their wet boots and wet swimsuits. Together they followed a path back down to the lake to retrieve the Tuckers' personal pack. Then they went back for the canoe, dumping out the water, two-manning it up into the campsite and setting it down next to the Old Town and

Seliga. With this done, they set out on their search for fire-wood. Even though the previous campers had left a big stack of split firewood, they would need even more fuel to see them through the night.

The sun had moved lower in the western sky, but unlike most evenings, the hot, dry, south wind continued to blow. High above them, the red pine branches swept back and forth, back and forth against the evening sky, whispering loudly as if praying for rain. As Danny followed his father back into the forest, he guessed that this would be another night of sleeping on the rocks beneath the stars. The women would have the tent. But at least they were safe. No one had drowned.

"What are we going to do?" he asked his father when they were out of earshot from the campsite.

"I don't know." Hank seemed irritated. "This is no place for the out-of-shape and the ill-prepared. Don't these people know that there are a hundred ways to die up here? Look what happened to us last year, with you and me and Mike... and we're experienced campers." He snapped dry branches off a downed red pine and stacked them on Danny's out-stretched arms. "I can't believe they lost their tent and food pack." Hank broke more branches with his feet. "I'm not sure what we're going to do. I just hope that big guy doesn't up and die on us tonight."

"Maybe you and I could go for help." Danny suggested tentatively.

"That may be the plan." Hank looked at him with a grim expression on his face. "That may well turn out to be the plan. I'll have to talk it over with your mother." Then he motioned for Danny to head back to the campsite with his load of firewood.

When they returned to the campsite Danny dropped his armload of wood near the fire pit. His swimsuit and boots had dried on the walk in the woods. Hank dropped his wood, too, and started to light the fire. Maddy and Anne Tucker had strung a long rope between four reddish tree trunks and were hanging up the wet sleeping bags and clothing from the Tuckers' drenched personal pack. Rachel was helping.

The girl, Julie, was standing beside her father, who was asleep now. She was wearing Danny's navy blue sweatshirt and sweatpants—the ones he used for pajamas on the trail. Danny walked over to her. She stood as tall as he stood. He guessed she was a ninth or tenth grader. "Hi, I'm Dan Forester. I guess I really haven't introduced myself." He reached out his right hand.

"I'm Julie Tucker." She shook his hand and let go—no sign of bruised fingers. "Thanks for rescuing us."

"Yeah, somehow we seem to find ourselves in these situations on our family canoe trips." Danny shrugged his shoulders as if rescuing swamped campers was a daily routine for the Foresters. "How's your dad?"

"Resting okay, I guess. Your mom says he's stable, but shouldn't move. The pain has stopped. It may have been a heart attack, but we're not sure how serious. We still need to get him to a hospital as soon as we can."

"I know," Danny said. "Where are you guys from?"

"Ohio. How about you all, where are you from?"

"Minneapolis." Then Danny thought he better tell her, because he worried about looking younger than his age. "I'm going into eighth grade," he said.

"Me, too." Julie smiled a bit—a beautiful smile.

Danny understood immediately—she was one of those girls in his grade who "matured early"—who looked about two or three years older than most of the boys in eighth grade. He knew at once that she was one of the popular girls—popular with teachers and coaches and all the other kids. She was one of those girls in his grade who sat at the lunchroom table with all the other popular kids.

He was one of those boys in eighth grade who might be mistaken for a seventh grader. He hadn't even started to shave yet, but hoped he looked at least thirteen. He was one of the band kids, not out for any sport. In the school lunchroom he sat with the computer geeks and the guys in chess club, talking about movies and video games. He knew exactly his place up against the likes of Julie Tucker. Except for one thing—her artificial arm. With that arm he couldn't quite imagine her sitting at the popular kids' table in the lunchroom. He didn't quite know where to fit her in the junior high school scheme of things. Not thinking, he glanced down at her left hand.

"I bet you're wondering how I lost my arm." Julie had caught his glance. "It's okay, everyone stares at first."

Danny stammered, embarrassed, "I… I'm sorry. I didn't mean to stare."

"I had a rare form of bone cancer when I was four, so they had to amputate my lower arm and hand."

Danny wasn't sure what to say next.

"Danny," Hank called out, "I could use some help with dinner."

"I gotta' go help my dad. Your father's going to be okay. My parents are like the world's best campers. We'll get him out of here in the morning, first thing."

"I hope so." Julie Tucker knelt again beside her father. Danny turned to help his dad with dinner.

Hank Forester threw together something he called Lac La Croix Stew, a mix of chicken and rice in a thick gravy simmering over the fire. Then he fried up a batch of bannock while a spice cake baked in the reflector oven. Danny hydrated a package of freeze-dried applesauce to go with the cake, and stirred up a fresh pot of lemonade. Finished with these tasks, he spread out the red and white checkered tablecloth on the ground and set out an assortment of plates, cups and silverware for six people. This done, he called everyone to gather around.

With the sun nearly set in the west, the Foresters and their unexpected guests, Anne and Julie Tucker, stood beneath the whispering red pines of Wounded Paw Peninsula. Bill Tucker lay sleeping behind them. Maddy and Rachel led them in singing the Johnny Appleseed grace.

Oh, the Lord is good to me,
And so I thank the Lord,
For giving me, the things I need,
The sun and the rain and the apple seed.
Oh, the Lord is good to me.

For Danny, there was something very comforting about the light of the fire and the smell of the wood smoke. And on this day, he felt more grateful than he could recall feeling in a long time for the good food his father had prepared—or more hungry. He hurriedly wolfed down the tasty stew and slurped his bug juice. Looking up from his cup he saw Julie Tucker staring at him. *Lunchroom*, he thought. *I'm at the geek table.*

"So, tell us how you came to be swamped out on Lac La Croix?" Hank asked Anne Tucker as they all sat on a circle of logs, eating their dinner.

"Bill came up here when he was a kid, with the Boy Scouts." She was wearing one of Maddy's cotton turtlenecks and a pair of her jeans. "He always talked about wanting to go back to the Boundary Waters. He kept his map from the Boy Scout trip and wanted to retrace the route they had taken. He even saved his old paddle. So, this summer we decided to try it." She looked over at her husband. Maddy stood up and walked over to check on Bill, still asleep on the ground.

"We started out on the Little Indian Sioux River. The water was lower than Bill remembered, and the portages were longer than he had remembered. It was all more difficult than we had planned for, or maybe we are just more out of shape than we thought. Anyway, we really struggled, but the first night we made it to Lynx Lake." She pulled her dark hair back into a ponytail as she talked.

"Yesterday we pushed on to Green Lake, two more long portages, five in all. Beautiful lakes, but last night we were exhausted. I even asked Bill about turning around and heading back. He said to see how I felt in the morning. When we woke up this morning we saw the smoke from the forest fire to the west."

Hank broke in, "That fire isn't even in the Boundary Waters. It's on the western side of Crane Lake."

"But we didn't know that," Anne Tucker continued her story. "We thought we were trapped, that maybe the fire was on the Little Indian Sioux River, so we pushed on to Gebeonequet Lake today, thinking we'd take Gebeonequet Creek into Lac La Croix. That was the route Bill had marked on his old Boy Scout map. But when we tried heading up the creek there was no water. It was all just muskeg and beaver dams. No other campers were around." Anne Tucker started to cry.

"We were stuck in muskeg up to our thighs," Julie helped her mother with the story, her arm around her mother's back. "There was no way we could have made it down that creek. We really thought we were trapped."

"So Bill got the idea to bushwhack overland to Lac La Croix." Anne started again. "We looked at the map. It seemed like the only option, to head due east through the forest to the lake. Bill led with the canoe, but about halfway across he started to feel sick, like indigestion. So there we were, in the middle of the woods, with no path to follow, just the compass needle pointing east. He wrestled with the canoe the whole way, getting it stuck between trees, falling. A couple of times all three of us had to lift it over windfalls. It took us all afternoon. Finally, we saw the lake, but we didn't know where exactly we were on the lake. We were lost."

Julie continued with the story. "When we got to the shore of the lake we had to lower the canoe and our gear and ourselves down a sort of a cliff into the water, with the waves pounding us. We almost swamped right there." She looked over at her father and Maddy. "Dad really looked sick. He said his arms hurt. But there was no good place to camp right there, and nothing to do but try to find a campsite. So, we just paddled out onto Lac La Croix looking for a campsite. We didn't realize the waves were so high. Dad was working really hard in the stern. Then he just sort of keeled over. The waves took his old Boy Scout paddle right out of his hands."

Danny added a few sticks to the fire. Night was settling in but the wind was not settling down.

"And you all know the rest." Anne Tucker finished the story.

"He's awake," Maddy reported. Everyone moved to Bill Tucker's side.

"How are you feeling?" Anne asked.

"Better, thanks to Dr. Forester." He looked up at Maddy and Hank. "So what's the plan?" he asked.

Hank answered. "In the morning, at first light, Danny and I will paddle north across Lac La Croix to the ranger station on the Indian reserve. They'll call for an air ambulance. A big orange helicopter's gonna' drop down right here, pick you folks up and fly you outta' here by about noon tomorrow."

"Praise God and the Foresters from Minnesota!" Julie hugged her mother. They both started crying, tears of joy and relief.

Danny stepped back to the fire, thinking. This was the

first he had heard about him and his father paddling north at first light. He looked out over the lake, listening to the sound of the waves against the rocks. Above him he could hear the tall red pines sweeping the sky with their thirsty branches, still praying for rain. It was night. *Why isn't the wind dying down?* He wondered. *Missepishu,* came the answer in his mind, *angry Missepishu.*

chapter four

WINDBOUND

D anny and his father worked by the light of the fire, preparing for their morning paddle north across Lac La Croix. First they took some rope and the kitchen tarp and constructed a lean-to over Bill Tucker. Maddy had already covered him with Hank's dry sleeping bag. The night wind and smoke from the fire would keep the mosquitoes away.

"Give him a few sips of water when he's thirsty, but no solid food." Maddy left her doctor's orders. "I'll be out to check on him every hour or two."

Bill Tucker was awake, sitting up higher with his back against the tree trunk. Anne Tucker kissed her husband on his forehead and Julie gave her father a hug, then both women, exhausted, headed into the tent. Rachel was already asleep. Maddy followed, zipping the tent door shut behind her.

Danny and Hank had changed into long pants, long-sleeved shirts and their campsite shoes. They dried their boots and trail socks next to the fire. Hank said they would take turns resting during the night, but Danny knew his father was not likely to sleep much.

Danny had thought that last year's two broken legs might dampen his father's spirit for camping. To the contrary, Hank Forester seemed invigorated and renewed by his near-death experience, even with a stainless steel rod screwed into one leg. All winter long he had pursued a rigorous routine of physical therapy—exercising, losing fat and gaining muscle. By June, the only sign of his injuries was a slight limp when he walked.

Danny, too, had changed physically. He had grown at least four inches, and looked almost skinny compared to his flabby self from a year earlier. He'd probably never become a star high school athlete like Mike had been, but at least he was no longer nearly the weakest kid in gym class.

"So what kind of work do you do in Ohio?" Hank asked Bill Tucker as he handed him a cup of water.

"I teach junior high English and reading." Bill sat up a bit higher and sipped water from the sierra cup.

"Really," Hank sounded surprised, "I'm a teacher, too. I teach oil painting at an art school. And I do some of my own work in a studio at our home."

"What do you like to paint?"

"Oh, it varies from year to year. Lately I've been working on a series of black bear paintings." Hank looked at Danny. Danny knew he was thinking about their trip from a year ago, and their encounter with a black bear that wandered into their campsite one night.

"Tell me, what does Anne do?"

"She's a financial analyst for a bank, a big bank, lots of responsibility. Lucky me, she makes twice as much as I do. You can't raise a family on a teacher's salary." Bill shook his head. "It was hard to find time for this trip. They don't like her to be away from the office."

"It seems we have more in common than I realized." Hank poked at the fire with a crooked stick. "One more question... do you ever teach any Robert Service poems?"

"Absolutely! He's my favorite northwoods poet." Hank's question seemed to perk up Bill. "I've memorized a bunch of his poems—"The Cremation of Sam McGee," "The Shooting of Dan McGrew," "The Call of the Wild." But my favorite Robert Service poem of all is ..."

"The Men That Don't Fit In," both Hank and Bill spoke at once, chuckling as they started to recite the poem from memory.

> *There's a race of men that don't fit in,*
> *A race that can't stay still;*
> *So they break the hearts of kith and kin,*
> *And they roam the world at will.*

After he finished the fourth verse of his recitation, Bill held his hand to his head. "I feel a little dizzy." He let the sierra cup drop to the ground.

"You better lie back down and stay quiet." Hank helped him get comfortable on the sleeping pad beneath the lean-to. Soon, Bill Tucker was back asleep.

Hank strapped down the food pack and set it against a large boulder. With an all-night fire burning, there was no need to hang the pack from a tree to prevent a bear raid. On this night they would break the seven o'clock-to-midnight open fire rule—this was an exception—an emergency.

"Let's look at the map." Hank spread the map of Lac La Croix out in the ground beside the fire. Danny added a few sticks of wood to the flames and knelt down next to his father. "We're here, on the American side." Hank pointed to his Wounded Paw Peninsula. "And we want to get to here." He pointed to a bay, north-by-northwest, on the Canadian side of the lake.

Danny read the words on the map, "Lac La Croix First Nation."

Hank explained. "That's the Indian reserve that abuts the western edge of the Quetico Park. It's a small band of Ojibwe folk, maybe three hundred total. About a hundred and fifty live on the reservation. They manage the park ranger station for the Lac La Croix entry points. The Quetico Park is just like the BWCAW. We'll have to get an entry permit. I already have our Remote Area Border Crossing permit from Canadian Customs, allowing us to enter into Canada."

By the light of the fire Danny studied the map—narrows, islands, and a vast open stretch of water, maybe three miles across. This wide stretch would be the most difficult part of the trip if the wind came up too early. But he trusted his father to guide the crossing.

Before dark they had set their paddles and life jackets down by the shoreline, next to the red Seliga. Tomorrow they would travel light, taking only a trail lunch, a water bottle, two sierra cups, compass, map, customs papers and the clothes on their backs. Hank folded up the map and slipped it into a clear plastic map case. Then he organized his rucksack. He would leave behind his sketchbook, box of pencils, Robert Service poetry book, camera, binoculars, Rachel's Birder's Ear and her loon whistle. Danny would remember to take along his Swiss army knife and his ten-in-one compass device, hanging from a lanyard around his neck.

"Why don't you try to get some sleep. I'll wake you later." Hank motioned for his assistant to find a spot on the ground against a fire circle log. He handed him two rain jackets, one to lie on and the other to cover up with. "We might as well get some use out of these, if it's not going to rain."

Danny spread one of the jackets out on the ground beside the log. Then he lay down, like an animal bedding down for the night, and pulled the other jacket on top of himself. The fire burned low, glowing red. Above him, he could see the twinkling of stars and the moon rising from the southeast. A great gray owl swooped low between the massive tree trunks, disappearing without a sound. The wind had quieted only slightly. The high pine branches with their long, finger-like needles continued scratching the night sky for water. Soon, resting his head on a stubby half-log of birch, he fell hard asleep.

Just as hard he was abruptly awakened by the sound of his mother's voice. "Bill," she spoke firmly, "is there any pain?" Danny sat up, blinking. He could see Bill Tucker turned on his side, throwing up, sick somehow. Hank was adding wood to the fire for more light.

"I'm okay, I'm okay," Bill reassured Maddy, wiping his sleeve across his mouth. "I just felt nauseated when I woke up."

"Let me have a listen." Maddy placed her stethoscope on Bill's chest, above his heart. "I wish I had my lab technicians and an EKG machine. We could use some test results. I want you to just continue to rest. Stay flat on your back." She glanced over her shoulder at Hank, a serious look on her face. "Here, take a sip of water. See if it stays down." She handed Bill a cup of water.

In the light of the fire Danny could see beads of sweat across the big man's face.

He turned to his father. "How soon before we go?" It was still very dark out.

"Not for another couple of hours. Why don't you lie back down and grab some more shut-eye." Hank's unshaven face looked even darker than usual, animal-like.

Danny laid his head back down on his log pillow and closed his eyes, wondering if he had been dreaming. But the first light of dawn came soon enough. In the middle of a real dream, Hank nudged him awake.

"Rise and shine, camper. We've got some serious paddling ahead of us." Danny opened his eyes to the faint light of the pre-dawn—just enough light to see without a fire. He sat up, rubbed his eyes, then stood up stiffly, his joints and muscles sore from the rescue ordeal the day before and from another night of sleeping on the hard ground. Hank handed him a cup of cocoa and a bowl of hot oatmeal topped with brown sugar and dried fruit. "This will stick with you—energy food."

Maddy was up, too, kneeling beside Bill with her stethoscope. He was still asleep, breathing heavily. She turned to her son and husband. "I don't want you taking any unnecessary risks out there. If the wind comes up early, don't try a crossing, just get back here and we'll find another way."

"Don't worry, Mom, we can do it." Danny tried to sound confident between spoonfuls of cereal. He was thinking about last year's trip, when he and Mike went off to find help for Hank, leaving him behind with two broken legs in a tent on Kahshahpiwi. This was just a six or seven mile paddle, with no portages and his dad with him. *What could go wrong?*

"Here." Hank handed Danny his dry boots and socks, a pair of trail shorts and a T-shirt. The sky was clear and the morning again unusually warm, promising an even hotter day than the day before. Danny changed into his paddling clothes and pulled on his boots. Hank grabbed his rucksack and headed for the canoe landing. Danny and his mother followed. No one else was awake.

Father and son two-manned the Seliga into the crystal clear water. Hank would paddle stern with Danny in the bow. But before they stepped into the canoe, Maddy waded into the water and gave Danny a hug. "You be careful," she cautioned.

"I will." Danny again tried to reassure his mother as he climbed into the bow.

"Hey, what about me?" Hank looked at Maddy.

"You be extra careful," she said seriously, pointing her finger at him as she sloshed out of the lake—no send-off hug for Hank. Danny could still feel the tension between his parents, but he put his worries about them out of his mind as he concentrated on the challenge in front of him—dangerous Lac La Croix. He tightened his PFD.

Out past the shelter of the cove the waves didn't look too bad, perhaps a bit choppy—no whitecaps. With a surge from Hank's big paddle they were off, not looking back. Danny could feel the intensity of his father's mood. He suspected his father had found his "bear mind"—remembering a conversation with him on last year's trip. Hank had explained that when he was faced with a tough physical challenge he would sometimes imagine himself as a wolf, a moose, an eagle or a bear—like Native American power animals. The ordeal ahead would require the strength of a bear.

They would paddle north across the open top of Lady Boot Bay, then into a narrows, around some islands and finally across the widest part of Lac La Croix. Hank paddled hard—a man on a mission. Danny settled into a steady bow stroke, pulling his broad paddle long and hard straight back, then feathering it flat against the water as he brought it forward.

"Good job, Dan-man," his father called out from behind him. "You're my best bowman ever."

"What about Mike?" Danny questioned his father's sincerity.

"Mike's a sternsman."

Danny wasn't sure what his father meant by this, but he was happy to have his approval. Away from the shelter of the cove they sliced through choppy waves with the warm south wind again at their backs. The sleek canoe gained momentum as Danny and his father hit their paddle strokes at precisely the same instant time after time.

"Switch sides whenever you get tired." Hank would let Danny set the pace.

Just as the sun rose fully above the tree line to the east, they crossed the place where they had pulled Bill Tucker out of the water the day before. Danny thought about Missepishu, the water panther, perhaps sleeping in the depths of Lac La Croix this morning, letting them pass unhindered. Even with his father paddling in the stern, Danny felt puny and vulnerable up against the power of this biggest of all Boundary Waters lakes. He pulled harder with his paddle to move them quickly past Missepishu's underwater lair.

So they progressed steadily north-by-northwest to where the open bay narrowed between the points of two big, tree-covered islands. Here the wind picked up, even this early in the day, as it pressed between the two islands. The first white-caps appeared in front of them. Danny knew they would have to hurry to beat the wind across the lake. There would be no time to rest.

Hank guided them through the narrows. More islands and more narrows lay ahead. Danny could feel his father pushing harder and harder as his muscles warmed with paddling. Empty of packs, the canoe rode higher in the water, gliding at top speed. "Switch," Danny called out. "One... two... three... switch." Without breaking stride, father and son switched their paddling sides.

Closer to shore, as they passed through the narrows, the low water was even more evident. The high watermarks on the rocks and the yellow pollen lines were five or six feet above the present water level. In this low water Danny began to worry about lake-sharks and dead-heads. Lake-sharks were sharp rocks just below the surface and dead-heads were submerged logs. Both could tear open the bottom of a wood-and-canvas canoe, even break the cedar ribs and planking. It was the bowman's responsibility to watch out for these hazards and warn the sternsman to steer clear. Besides that, to be careless with one of the family's wooden canoes was nearly the worst of possible sins.

But faster and faster they paddled, sprinting across another open stretch of water before approaching a second narrows. They were now well out of sight of Wounded Paw Peninsula. As they approached the second narrows, Danny called back to his father in the stern, "Should I shotgun?" Shotgunning was when the bowman knelt forward in the bow, holding his paddle like a shotgun with the grip forward just under the water to ward off any lake-sharks, as the sternsman paddled slowly through lake-shark infested waters.

"No," Hank answered. "We should be okay through this stretch."

Danny could feel another surge of strength from his father's paddle. "Switch," he called out. "One... two... three..." but before he could say "switch" again, a hard jolt threw him forward in the bow and a terrible ripping, cracking sound cried up from the belly of the canoe. "Oh, no!" Danny felt sickened. He had failed to see the lake-shark.

"Hang on!" Hank shouted as they spilled sideways into the lake, the red canoe filling with cold lake water.

Danny hung onto the right gunwale of the swamped canoe and looked back at his father, bracing for an angry growl. But Hank Forester appeared strangely calm—a hairy bear out for a swim. He strapped his rucksack onto the stern thwart, then looked at Danny. "I know what you're think-ing... that this is your fault for not shotgunning. But you're wrong. This is my fault for pushing too hard and not being careful. Come on, let's swim it to shore."

So they stowed their paddles across the bow seat and swam the damaged Seliga toward shore, maybe forty yards away. They swam with the wind and waves, floating in their life jackets. Eventually they made their way to a narrow peb-ble beach, exposed only in the low water.

"Are you okay?" Hank asked Danny as they emptied the water out of the canoe and set it, belly up, on the beach.

"Yeah, I'm okay. But what about the canoe and what about Bill Tucker?"

"Maybe we can still make it. Let's assess the damage." Hank stepped up toward the bow of the canoe. There, just below the bow seat, an L-shaped tear in the canvas ran maybe eighteen inches. A section of the thin wood planking was smashed through and two ribs were cracked. The vessel could not be paddled without repair.

Hank shook his head. "I left my canoe repair kit back in the food pack... and I didn't even pack any matches." He sat down on the rocks with his back against the canoe. "This is all my fault. I was in a big hurry. I wanted to be the hero, maybe to show your mother that I could save lives, too. She's been mad at me all summer for letting Mike join another fire crew. I guess I was trying to get back into her good graces, but I forgot to respect the lake."

"What are we going to do?" Danny sat down next to his father, both looking out over the choppy blue water. They had not seen any other campers on that remote stretch of shoreline. They weren't even at a campsite. Behind them the forest was a thick tangle of white spruce, balsam fir and jack pine trees, cedar along the shoreline. Already, the south wind was on the rise, as the morning sun climbed higher in the sky. It was hot. Their chances of reaching the ranger station now seemed slim to none. "How is Mom going to know we didn't make it? The Tuckers will be looking for an orange helicopter." Danny felt terrible, a welling up of fear. He hung his head. "If Mike had been paddling bow, this wouldn't have happened."

"You don't know that, Danny. Come on. I have a plan." Hank stood up. He emptied everything out of his rucksack. The trail lunch had survived, sealed in a plastic bag. He set this under the canoe along with the bottle of cherry bug juice. Next he spread the wet map and the customs papers out in the sun to dry, holding them down with rocks. He propped the map case open with a stick to dry the inside of it in the wind. The compass was still attached with a lanyard. Finally, he handed Danny his stainless steel sierra cup by its wire handle. "Do you still have that magnifying glass on your ten-in-one compass devise?"

"Yeah," Danny nodded his head and held up the red plastic device—more like a kid's toy than a camping tool.

"Good, we'll use that to start a fire." Hank turned his rucksack inside out and set it on top of the canoe next to his life jacket. Danny took off his life jacket, too, and laid it on top of the canoe. "Follow me," Hank motioned inland. "Our clothes will dry as we walk." Then he grabbed his own sierra cup and headed into the thick forest. Danny followed without talking, pushing aside branches.

About forty yards inland from the rocky beach, Hank found two old balsam fir trees standing side by side. "See here." He showed Danny the blisters of sap all up and down the greenish-brown tree trunks. "We can fill our cups with balsam sap, cook it thick over a fire and use it to seal up that tear in the canvas." Hank held his sierra cup up next to the tree trunk and popped one of the blisters. A sticky sap squirted into his cup. "Work from top to bottom."

"Are you sure this will work?" Danny worried about losing even more time on some hairbrained scheme of his father's.

"Sure I'm sure. Get going."

So Danny started popping blisters of sap into his cup. Sometimes the sap would squirt sideways all over his hand. He wondered how he was ever going to get the sticky mess washed off. "Man, I'm getting this all over me," he complained to his father.

"I know. We're going to smell like Christmas trees for about a month. Just keep at it."

Blister by blister, fingers covered with sap, it took nearly an hour for the shipwrecked rescuers to fill their cups with the pine-scented tree sap. Back at the beach they carefully set their gooey cupfuls of sap under the canoe. Then they set about building a fire.

"Get out your magnifying glass." Hank arranged a small circle of rocks in the sun, using the canoe as much as possible as a shelter from the wind. Danny noticed that the wind had come up higher by now, whitecaps showing even in the narrows. He didn't say anything about the wind to his dad. Certainly they both knew that it was getting too late to cross the widest part of Lac La Croix. Talking about it wasn't going to help. For the moment, they had to concentrate on patching the canoe.

Hank carefully constructed a teepee of tinder in the middle of the fire rocks. He had even found some small shreds of birchbark—the best fire starter. "Okay, do your thing."

Danny knelt by the tinder. He opened up his ten-in-one compass device and found the small magnifying glass, wiping the lens on his shirt. "What if it doesn't work?" He looked up at his father.

"It'll work," Hank reassured him.

Danny positioned the lens in the sun, holding it steady. He aimed the yellow-red spot of hot concentrated sunlight right on the birchbark shreds. And sooner than he had imagined, in about thirty seconds, the tinder began to smoke. A few seconds later a flame appeared. "Hey! It worked!" He laughed out loud.

"Good man!" Hank patted him on the back. Together they carefully added more tinder to the flame until a fire took hold. Then they added sticks of pine, building up a small campfire in the rocks next to the canoe—at the same time violating a number of U.S. Forest Service fire safety rules. But Danny didn't care. This was an emergency. They had to get back to Maddy, Rachel and the Tuckers. Without saying it, he knew it was too late for them to cross Lac La Croix to the north. They should have made it to the ranger station by now.

Hank placed two thick sticks of green wood parallel an inch or two apart across the middle of the fire. Carefully, he set both sap-filled sierra cups on the sticks over the flames to thicken into balsam pitch. The sap heated up slowly, bubbling and bubbling. Danny kept the fire fed with small sticks. Finally, when it was ready, Hank used two short sticks like a pair of tongs to lift the hot cups of pitch out of the fire. With

Danny's knife, he had whittled another stick flat, like a putty knife. "Use this to spread the pitch as I pour it on the tear." He handed the flat stick to Danny.

Working together, Hank poured the first cup of hot glue on the canvas tear. Danny spread it and smoothed it with his putty knife stick. He repeated his work as Hank poured the second cup of pitch over the seam. There was just enough pitch to cover the torn canvas.

"Let it cool and harden." Hank handed Danny the bottle of bug juice and opened their trail lunch—gorp, licorice, cheese, beef jerky, crackers and some of Maddy's homemade energy bars she called "voyageur bars." It all tasted like balsam sap as they ate with their fingers. Their sierra cups were ruined for drinking, so they drank straight from the water bottle, sitting again with their backs against the canoe, looking out over the lake.

They had started out at about six o'clock. If everything had gone as planned, they could have made it to the ranger station by about eight o'clock, just ahead of the wind. But the swamping had cost them nearly an hour. The hike into the woods and sap collecting took another hour. The fire building, pitch making and canoe repair ate up one more hour. Now, it was nearly ten o'clock and they were still waiting for the pitch to harden.

"I guess we switch to Plan B." Hank spoke as he chewed on a piece of licorice.

"What's that?" Danny hoped his father hadn't conjured up some bizarre bushwhacking scheme.

"We head back to the campsite. If we get there by noon your mother and the Tuckers shouldn't be too worried about the helicopter not arriving yet."

Danny felt relieved. "What's Plan C?" he asked.

"I don't know. Maybe a night paddle." Hank looked out over the lake. "We'll have to talk that over with Maddy and the Tuckers." He stood up, stiffly, to inspect their canvas repair job. "Looks good. Let's give it a try."

Just then Danny spotted something washed up on the beach about a hundred feet away. He ran down the shoreline to check it out. "It's Bill Tucker's Boy Scout paddle," he called back to his father, lifting the painted paddle above his head.

"Bring it here." Danny ran back to the canoe. Hank examined the old paddle with Bill Tucker's name wood-burned on the shaft. "All right! At least Bill will be happy about this."

Together they rolled the damaged Seliga over on its belly and set it in the water with the bow pointed back toward the south.

"Any leaks?" Hank asked Danny.

Danny examined the cracked ribs and planking. "Doesn't look like it."

"Okay, hold it right there."

Danny stood knee deep in the water beside the canoe as Hank collected the map, compass, customs papers, rucksack and sierra cups. He threw Danny his PFD. Then he poured four bottles of water on the fire, feeling the ashes with his hands to make sure they were absolutely out cold. To finish the job, he covered the ashes with sand and pebbles from the beach, erasing all evidence of a fire.

"Let's go, camper." Hank held the canoe steady as Danny again stepped into the bow, this time facing into the hot wind. "Paddle hard, now. We'll rest behind that first island, but once we head back out into the open there'll be no stopping."

A gust of wind slapped a wave against the side, spraying water on Danny. He knew this promised to be a wet crossing. He hoped the patched canvas beneath his feet would hold up. Hank climbed back into the stern seat and shoved off with the grip of his paddle. "Switch on three whenever you want to." Danny nodded. Again they found their rhythm, this time into the wind, hot sun beating down. Eleven o'clock—they reached the lee of the first island as the wind began to peak.

"This is gonna' be worse than yesterday with the Tuckers." Hank talked. Danny listened, head down, resting his paddle across his legs. The canoe bobbed in the waves even though they were sheltered momentarily from the wind. "When we get out into it, we better switch every ten strokes, just like last year paddling into Cache Bay." Danny recalled the pain of that ordeal. Even though he had become a stronger paddler, he was not looking forward to this sprint into the wind. "This is one of those tests you said you wanted, so choose your beast—wolf-moose-eagle-bear." Hank dug his paddle deep into the lake and steered the sturdy Seliga past the island, angling south into wind and waves.

Danny understood the meaning of his father's words. He could feel the blade of his paddle bend as he, too, dug hard into the water. "Eight... nine... ten... switch!" he called out after his first ten strokes. By now he could see Wounded Paw Peninsula across the water on the south shore of the American side. Splash! Splash! Splash! The biggest waves came at them in sets of three, hitting hard at the belly of the bow, just like the crossing of Lake Saganaga last year. "Eight... nine... ten... switch!" he called out again, groaning with each pull of his paddle. *I can do this,* he thought to himself. *I can make it. Don't quit. Don't ever quit.*

But these were waves like no waves Danny had ever seen before—maybe four feet high. Splash! Splash! Splash! Big three-set after big three-set hit again and again. Luckily they rode high in the empty canoe. Hank held them steady, square to the wind. His greater weight in the stern kept the bow up. So, amazingly, they took on almost no water as the high bow split each wave. The danger would come if they ever shoveled the front end into a wave.

Then in the middle of the worst of it, from behind him, Danny could hear his father bellowing out one of his corny, made-up Robert Service poems:

> *There's a father and son who can't be beat,*
> *In crossing Lady Boot Bay.*
> *They've never lost or known defeat,*
> *In camping the Forester way.*
> *They'll find a way to rescue Bill,*
> *To their promise they'll hold true.*
> *By power of muscle or strength of will,*
> *They'll see the mission through.*

"Ha!" Hank laughed into the wind.

But we have failed, Danny thought to himself. *How are we going to explain this to Mom and the Tuckers?* Splash! Splash! Splash! This time Danny noticed more water in the bottom of the canoe. "Eight... nine... ten... switch!" He looked down at his feet, beneath the bow seat. There he could see a steady trickle of water leaking into the canoe from underneath one of the cracked ribs. "We've sprung a leak!" he shouted over his shoulder.

"Just keep paddling," came the order from his father.

Shoulders aching, arms tiring, Danny remembered Mike's advice—to brace his feet and pull back with his whole upper body, not just his arms and shoulders. Danny repositioned his legs and pulled hard with his back. "Eight... nine... ten... switch!" Steadily they progressed, leaning into the wind, pulling harder and harder with each stroke until at last they caught some of the lee shelter of the tree line to the south— the worst of it behind them.

Danny looked up. He could see the four women, Maddy, Rachel, Anne and Julie, standing out on the rocky tip of the peninsula, watching them. Maddy held Hank's binoculars.

Rachel had her Birder's Ear. Still, it was another half an hour before they entered the wind-sheltered cove. Both men dropped their paddles, drifting to shore, their energy spent. About three inches of lake water sloshed about in the bottom of the leaking red canoe. Maddy waded out to catch the bow at the landing.

"It's my fault," Danny blurted out. "I should have seen the lake-shark."

"No, it's not, Danny." Hank stepped into the water. He looked at Maddy. "I was pushing it too hard. I should have slowed down through the narrows. We caught a rock, tore the belly, broke two ribs and swamped. If it hadn't been for Danny's magnifying glass, we'd still be out there." He looked at Anne and Julie Tucker. "I'm very sorry about this, but for now, we're windbound." Then with a groan he flipped up his precious Seliga, dumping the water onto himself, and carried it, limping stiffly, up into the campsite.

Danny caught a glimpse of Julie Tucker's unhappy face. Quickly he collected all three paddles and followed his father up the granite slope to the campsite.

"I like your wood canoe," Bill Tucker spoke almost cheerfully, appearing unconcerned about the rescuers' failed attempt to make it to the ranger station. He was sitting up against the tree where Hank and Danny had left him.

Hank flipped down, carefully placing the damaged Seliga belly up on a bed of pine needles. "I'm sorry we didn't make it, Bill, but Danny found your Boy Scout paddle and I made up a Robert Service poem for you. That's all we can offer you today—no orange helicopter. So how are you feeling?" he asked as he walked past Bill's lean-to, not stopping.

"Better, but the doctor says I still have to rest." Bill looked up at Hank. "How are you feeling?"

"Honestly, I'm pretty tired." The big man continued on his way to the hammock he had strung back and away from the fire pit. He sat down in the middle of it and pulled off his wet boots and socks. Then he laid back into the netting and stretched out his legs. In less than a minute he was asleep, swaying back and forth in the wind. It had been a day and a half since he had slept.

Danny, hanging his head, looking dispirited, handed Bill Tucker his old Boy Scout paddle.

"Thank you, Danny."

"You mean thanks for nothing." He threw his life jacket on the ground, plopped down on top of it and proceeded to unlace his wet boots. What he had hoped would be a fun family adventure had turned into a grueling ordeal, a grinding test of strength and endurance. His whole body hurt. But worse than that, he felt like a loser in the eyes of Julie Tucker—just another kid at the geek table in the junior high lunchroom. That was the part that hurt worse than his body. He heaved one of his heavy wet boots toward the fire pit. It landed in the ashes.

chapter five

NIGHT PADDLE

Maddy Forester called a meeting beneath the big fire-scarred red pine. Everyone except Hank gathered around Bill, sitting on the ground. Maddy spoke. "Here's the situation. Like it or not we are windbound. I don't understand this hot wind coming from the south because the prevailing wind up here comes out of the northwest. But it looks we're stuck with it, at least for now." She looked mostly at Anne and Bill Tucker. "There's no sense in trying to head east, that's just fifty more miles of wilderness. You folks bushwhacked in from the west, so we know that's impassable. We could possibly head back south, back up the Moose River, but that involves about eight portages."

Then she talked more directly to her patient. "Bill, I don't want you up walking around, much less paddling and portaging. You may feel better now, but patients always feel better in the morning, then worse as the day goes on. I'm still not certain what happened to you out on the lake, but I don't want to take any chances with your health." A dead branch broke loose high above in the wind and dropped to the ground. "I still think the best plan is to try to make it north to the Quetico Park ranger station. It's an all-water route, only six or seven miles. We could do it tonight, under the full moon. But I don't want to act like the Foresters are a bunch of know-it-alls. The Tucker family has some say in this, too." Maddy ended her speech.

Bill and Anne and Julie Tucker looked at each other. Julie shrugged her shoulders. "I don't know. I just want to get out of here."

"What about some kind of a signal fire?" Anne asked.

Maddy shook her head. "For a signal fire to be seen, it would have to be a very big, smoky fire. With this wind, in these dry conditions, I don't want to be responsible for a fire getting out of control and burning down half the Boundary Waters."

"Do you think there might be anyone else on the lake who could help us? Maybe someone has a cell phone or someone could go for help?" Julie offered her ideas.

"We are likely out of reach for any cell phones, and everyone else on this lake is windbound, too. We could end up wasting a lot of time and energy chasing around the lake and not finding anyone any better equipped than we are to go for help. Believe me, if Hank Forester turned back, then it has to be pretty bad out there." Maddy made eye contact with Danny.

Bill Tucker spoke up. "Hey, after what happened yesterday I'm just happy to still be alive and with my family and in the care of Dr. Forester. I vote for the night paddle."

Anne Tucker agreed. "Don't worry about taking charge, Maddy. We appreciate your leadership in this situation."

Maddy collected nods of agreement from everyone. "Okay, then... a night paddle it is. Anne and I will organize the packs and cook dinner. Later on, Danny and Rachel can take down the tent. When Hank wakes up, he'll fix the red canoe with his fiberglass repair kit. But for now, I need you kids to do something for me."

"What's that?" Danny asked.

"See if you can find some blueberries. Even in this drought, there should still be some berries out there. I want to bake a pie."

"All right, blueberry picking!" Rachel jumped up in excitement, breaking the grim tone of the meeting. She grabbed Julie by the hand. "Come on."

Julie looked at her mother. "Go ahead," Anne encouraged her.

"I'll need six cups of berries, plus some more firewood." Maddy made sure Danny understood the assignment.

Rachel was already digging into the food pack for extra plastic food bags. She found one each for herself, Julie and her brother. She and Julie headed up the forest path leading away from the campsite. Danny hustled to put on his dry campsite shoes and chase after them. A red squirrel chattered loudly to warn other squirrels about the three intruders hiking into their territory.

"So where do we find blueberries?" Julie asked Rachel as they walked together.

Danny answered from behind them. "We have to get out of this stand of red pine and find some open sunny areas, maybe up on a rocky ridge. Follow me." He skipped past the girls and stepped up the pace along the fern-lined trail. As he walked, he looked for signs of wildlife besides chattering squirrels, maybe a fisher or pine martin. But in the windy heat of the day, he knew that most animals were lying low.

About a quarter mile farther south, the trail led up hill and opened into a wide rock outcropping. In some places the weathered granite was covered with pale, gray-green lichen.

In other places deep patches of reindeer moss spread out over
the open surface. The moss was so dry it crunched under
their feet as they walked, leaving deep footprints. Growing in
between the lichen and the moss, patches of low bush blueberry shrubs showed their dark green leaves.

"This is what we're looking for." Danny made his first eye
contact with Julie Tucker. He was relieved to see that the
unhappy expression had left her face. All three of them
squatted down by the shrubs, looking for the delicious
berries.

"I see some. They're small, but good enough." Rachel was
ever enthusiastic. "If we work at it we can find enough for a
pie."

"How do you bake a pie on the trail?" Julie asked as she
started picking berries.

"It's easy," Danny explained, "we use a reflector oven.
You'll see when we get back to the campsite." He popped a
few juicy berries into his mouth.

"Hey, don't eat any!" Rachel protested, punching Danny

on the arm.

"Shut up, brat. I can eat as many as I want to. There's a whole forest of blueberries here."

Still, it took them a long while to gather enough berries for a pie. After about an hour the three berry pickers took a break, sitting on a patch of moss. Danny noticed that Julie had switched the hand on her prosthetic left arm to a stainless steel gripper. With her left-handed gripper she held open her plastic bag. With her right hand she picked berries. He didn't say anything about her hand, but that didn't stop Rachel from blathering on. "That's pretty cool, the way you can change the attachments on your hand... sort of like Inspector Gadget." Rachel pointed to Julie's arm.

"Rachel," Danny scowled, feeling embarrassed by her forwardness. He looked at Julie. "Do you have a rubber bat attachment for whacking big-mouthed little sisters?"

"It's okay, Dan. I'd rather have people ask questions than pretend they don't see me." Then she looked at Rachel. "Actually, I have a number of attachments for my arm, including one especially designed for working on the computer and one for swimming. I'm on the swim team at my school." She looked back at Danny. "I plan to study biomedical engineering in college." Then she set her bag of blueberries down and walked over to a place where the open rock met the tree line. Danny and Rachel continued gathering berries. Danny thought about telling Julie how he hoped some day to become a surgeon.

A few minutes later Julie returned with a fistful of delicate yellow and blue flowers. "I thought these might cheer up my dad."

"Oh, oh." Rachel shook her head. "You're not supposed to pick flowers. It's against the Forest Service rules."

"What?"

"It's okay, Rachel." Danny tried to shut her up. "You don't

have to be so rigid about the rules."

"Leave only footprints. Take only pictures. Isn't that our motto?" Rachel insisted on the rightness of her position.

"Don't listen to her, Julie. You can pick a few flowers back in the woods, away from the campsite, for your dad." He could see the expression of hurt on Julie's face.

"Where's my bag of blueberries," she asked, looking around on the ground where she thought she had left them. "They're gone. I can't find them."

"Probably a Maymaygwayshi took them." It was Rachel piping up again. "You shouldn't have left them unguarded."

"Shut up, Rachel." Now Danny could see that Julie was feeling even worse. Rachel had scolded her for picking flowers, and she had lost her bag of blueberries.

"Geez!" Julie threw down the flowers. "What am I even doing out here with you two. Maymaygwashi! Missepishu! Leave no trace!" Her blond hair blew across her face. "You all are some kind of crazy, fanatical northwoods ecology freaks. We should be home. My dad should be in a hospital. If it weren't for your stupid wood canoe and your stupid father we'd be outta' here by now. I hate this place!" She threw up her hands, turned and ran back down the path toward the campsite.

"Way to go, doofus, can't you see how worried she is about her father?" Danny handed his bag of berries to Rachel. "You carry the blueberries. I'll get some firewood." Standing up, he spotted Julie Tucker's bag of blueberries on the ground, partially hidden behind a rock. He picked them up and gave them to Rachel. In doing so he realized that Julie had picked about as many berries as Rachel and he had picked together. Rachel noticed this, too.

"I'm sorry, Danny." Rachel hung her head.

"Forget it, bird-girl." Danny put his arm on her shoulder as they walked back in the direction of the camp. "You just have to remember that not everyone up here camps the Forester way. You have to allow for some differences."

.   .   .

Back at the campsite Maddy Forester and Anne Tucker had organized the personal packs and repacked the food pack, leaving out what was needed for dinner. Bill was asleep again. Hank was up from his nap, working on the damaged Seliga. Julie Tucker was sitting on a large boulder with her back to everyone, looking out over the wind-swept lake. Rachel handed her mother the bags of blueberries. Danny dropped a huge armload of firewood on the ground, including half a dozen pine knots he had found.

"Thank you," Maddy acknowledged their work.

Suddenly Danny felt an overpowering fatigue set into his muscles. His mother could see the tiredness in him. She pointed to the hammock. Danny nodded and made his way to the nylon net strung between the trees. In two days he had exhausted himself on two separate rescue efforts in big wind and wild waves, sleeping on the ground for only a few hours in between. Now, all this exertion had caught up with him. He curled up in the hammock, leaving his shoes on. In less than a minute, like his father, he was asleep beneath the whispering pines, rocking in the wind like a child of the wilderness.

Four hours later Danny awoke to the smell of wood smoke and the sound of a crackling fire. The sun had moved lower in the sky. He guessed it was seven o'clock. He stood up and walked over to his parents by the canoes. Hank was putting the finishing touches on his repair of the red Seliga. Maddy was rolling out pie dough on the bottom of the green Old Town. She used a fuel canister from the camp stove as a rolling pin. They both looked up at him.

"Hey, camper, rested up enough for another paddle?" Hank asked.

"Yeah, I guess so," Danny answered, not quite awake.

He noticed that Bill Tucker's lean-to tarp had been returned to the kitchen area, and that he was no longer lying in his place beneath the fire-scarred red pine. For a moment he thought maybe he had been dreaming—maybe the Tucker family episode had all been just one big wild dream. He rubbed his eyes. Then he heard Rachel's playful voice from the direction of the lake. Looking down the granite slope to the water, he saw Rachel swimming in the wind-sheltered cove, along with Anne and Julie Tucker. Bill Tucker was lying back on the smooth rock, watching, as if to play lifeguard.

"How's Bill doing?" Danny asked.

Maddy shook her head. "Danny, I'm not a cardiologist, so I can't say for certain, but I don't like what I hear through my stethoscope from my patient's chest. We really need to get him to a hospital by tomorrow. Don't repeat that. I just want you to know how serious this is. We moved him out in the wind onto the rock to keep the mosquitoes off of him." She dumped her pot of sugared blueberries into the bottom crust of her pie pan. Then she constructed a lattice top. "Come on, help me bake this pie."

Danny set up Maddy's new reflector oven. This was essentially an aluminum shelf with two sides and a slanted roof. The whole thing could be folded flat and stored inside the food pack when not in use. Danny set it up in front of the open fire, making sure the shelf was level. Hank had taught him how to use the reflector oven on last year's Quetico trip. Hank could bake all kinds of breads and cakes, even pizza. But when it came to making pies, Maddy's perfection could not be matched.

"Be careful not to get the fire too hot," Maddy cautioned. "I don't want the top crust burned and the bottom crust

soggy." She lifted up the oven door and grabbed the hot pie pan with a pair of pliers, giving it a quarter turn. In reflector ovens, the part of the pie or cake closest to the flames always got done first, so the pan had to be turned every few minutes. Maddy hovered over her pie, watching it carefully. Slowly, the top crust began to brown and sweet blueberry juice began to ooze through the lattice windows.

"Hurray for blueberry pie!" Rachel shouted as she ran toward the fire.

Bill Tucker walked with one arm each around the shoulders of his wife and daughter. His face was white. He looked at Maddy. "You were right," he said, "your patient is feeling worse as the day wears on." Anne and Rachel helped him lie down again on Hank's sleeping pad beneath the red pine. Maddy brought him a cup of water and listened again to his chest with her stethoscope.

"I want everyone to change into the clothes and shoes they'll be wearing tonight. Then we can finish packing up and take down the tent. We'll keep the fire burning until midnight. After that, we'll all move down to the shore to wait until the wind dies down and the moon rises. I'm guessing the best time to start out will be about two o'clock. We should be able to reach the ranger station at daybreak." Hank nodded his agreement. Danny was happy to see his mother take charge of things.

Rachel and Anne and Julie ducked into the tent to change clothes. Danny noticed that Julie had removed her prosthetic arm for the swim in the lake. He was amazed by how unself-conscious she seemed to be about her disability. Watching her walk away he found himself imagining what it would be like to be her friend at school. *I bet she is popular,* he thought to himself, *really popular.* He understood that he was *likeable enough* at school—he got good grades and no one picked on him or anything—but he was not necessarily *popular. There's the difference,* he thought, *she's really popular... but I'm just like-able enough.* He turned to tend to his pie-baking fire.

Returning to the kitchen, Anne and Julie Tucker admired Maddy Forester's blueberry pie as it sat cooling on a tree stump. Being from Ohio, they understood the meaning of a good pie. "I cannot believe it." Anne smiled. "Out here in the middle of nowhere and you bake a pie that looks like something from my grandma's kitchen."

"Well, not exactly." Maddy pointed out the burnt edges of crust and pieces of ash that inevitably land on top of anything cooked in front of an open fire. "But it's not too bad for a trail pie."

For dinner Maddy and Anne cooked up a pot of chili-mac. Maddy helped Rachel and Julie bake two plates of golden cornbread in the reflector oven. Danny filtered more water from the lake and mixed a fresh bottle of bug juice. Hank took some of the water and made a pot of coffee. When it was time for dessert, Maddy cut her beautiful pie into six pieces. Bill was still on a liquid diet but was allowed a taste of the wild blueberry treat.

"Mmmm, that's good pie," he moaned with pleasure.

"Good everything," Danny chimed in. He ate ravenously, fueling his body for another push across the lake on little sleep.

Hank handed Julie her piece of blueberry pie on a blue enamelware plate. "Julie, I want to apologize to you for hitting you on your hand out on the lake yesterday. I was frightened and I overreacted."

Julie looked up at Hank. "That's okay, Mr. Forester, I understand." She glanced at Danny, then back to Hank. "I apologize for calling you stupid today." Hank raised his eyebrows and looked at Danny. He wasn't sure what Julie was talking about.

"It's all forgotten." Danny took another bite of pie.

"Well, let's get packed up." Maddy took charge again. She and Anne quickly washed the dishes in the big pot from the cook kit. Danny and Hank two-manned the wood canoes down to the shoreline. They would leave the Tucker's aluminum canoe behind for the outfitter to retrieve. Rachel and Julie collected the paddles and life jackets and set them down by the canoes. Then the four of them, Danny, Hank, Rachel and Julie, worked to take down the tent and finish packing the personal packs. When they were finished, Hank and Danny hauled the three personal packs and the food pack down to the shoreline by the canoes. The only things left out were a sleeping bag and pad for Bill to lie on in the canoe, their flashlights, Hank's rucksack and the cook kit by the fire pit. The two biggest pots would be used for water to put out the fire.

Night had fallen. For the first time in two days the wind had started to weaken with the setting sun. Hank said it would take a few hours for the waves to settle down. "Feel free to nap for a while," he quietly suggested, but no one looked like they were going to sleep. Everyone except Bill was sitting around the campfire, wearing jackets or sweatshirts, leaning back against logs or boulders, watching Danny's pine knots burn. No one offered to lead songs or tell a story. Out on the lake a loon cried out. "That's a good sign," Hank said to no one in particular. He added another pine knot to the fire. A spiral of white smoke twisted into the night sky.

.   .   .

Midnight came soon enough. Hank and Maddy poured water on the fire and stirred the ashes. Danny held the flashlight for the Tuckers as Anne and Julie walked Bill down to the canoes. Rachel carried Bill's sleeping pad and bag. Down by the lake Maddy again listened to Bill's chest. Hank showed up last with his rucksack and the old cook kit in its canvas bag. The stars sparkled intensely against the black night sky. A pale yellow moon peeked above the tree line to the southeast. Danny turned off his flashlight. Everyone's eyes adjusted to the night.

"Wow, look at the Milky Way." Bill Tucker laid his back against the smooth sloping granite, looking up at the clear night sky. "It's been nearly thirty years since I came up here as a Boy Scout. I've wanted to come back ever since, just for a night like this."

"Look, a falling star," Julie pointed above the horizon to the north.

"Make a wish, honey."

"I wish we all make it safely to the ranger station."

No one else spoke for a long while. Danny leaned back against one of the packs and dozed off. What seemed like only minutes later, Hank nudged him awake. "Time to go, camper." Hank and Maddy had floated the two canoes in the shallow water of the cove. Everyone donned their life jackets.

Hank lifted the pack Danny was resting against and placed it in the Old Town with two of the other packs. Then they started loading people.

First, Hank spread out the sleeping pad on the bottom of the Seliga. Then he carried Bill in his arms, sloshing through the water, and laid him down in the bow compartment, keeping him dry. Maddy stood knee-deep holding the canoe steady. Bill slid his head and shoulders under the yoke with his feet forward under the bow seat. Hank covered him with the sleeping bag.

Next Hank lifted Anne into the stern compartment. She sat cross-legged facing forward with her back against the smallest pack and Bill's head in her lap. Then Hank carried Rachel to the Old Town and set her in the bow compartment as the duffer. He had already positioned three packs in the stern compartment. By now Danny had waded into the lake and was holding onto the stern seat of the Old Town. Hank turned to Julie.

"I can get my feet wet." She waded into the cool water.

Danny handed her a paddle. "Switch sides whenever you want to, just call it out."

"I know how," she replied, and stepped carefully into the bow. "But it takes me a little extra time to position my left hand."

"That's okay, we won't be racing." Danny eased into the stern seat.

"Where's my Birder's Ear and my loon whistle?" Rachel reached a hand toward her father.

Hank opened his rucksack and pulled out Rachel's toys. "Here," he said, "but I want you to sit very still in the center of the canoe." Then he turned to Maddy. "Let's go, partner." She nodded. "Stay together, now," he called to Danny as he held the Seliga steady for Maddy to climb into the bow. Then he took the stern. And just like that, they were off—Hank

and Maddy, the old voyageurs, paddling the red Seliga—
Danny and Julie, the rookies, paddling the green Old Town.
They would follow the North Star by the light of the full
moon, moving in and out of the shadows cast by towering
pines.

The lake was quiet but not still. In the semi-darkness, as
they moved out over the deeper waters, Danny could feel the
slow, rhythmic rise and fall of the water beneath the belly of
the Old Town. It was as if the lake were deep-sleep breathing,
exhausted after days on end of battling the south wind, its
vast belly rising and falling against the bellies of the red and
green canoes. Maybe this is what Danny's father meant when
he said that the lake was like a living organism—a form of
life deserving respect—no soap in the water, no cans and bottles sunk to the bottom. Or maybe the water panther slept
this night as the respectful campers crossed over its underwater lair.

It was at this point that Maddy began the singing, quietly.
Anne joined in, then Julie, Rachel, Hank and Danny.

> *Hey-ho, anybody home*
> *Meat nor drink nor money have we none*
> *Still we will be merry*
> *Hey-ho, anybody home*

They sang the old camp song as a round, quietly, over
and over until they reached the narrows between the two big
islands Hank and Danny had paddled through the previous
morning. Here they moved deeper into the moon shadows.
Hank and Maddy in the lead slowed to a glide. "It's a deep
channel." Danny could hear his father talking to his mother.
"It's the narrows up ahead where we swamped." The canoes
slipped through the water with hardly a ripple.

As the lake widened again, Rachel lifted her loon whistle

and blew a perfect-sounding loon cry, sent drifting across the water, then another and another. She paused. In a moment her bird-kin responded, crying out to her beneath the silver moon. She called out again, this time with her tremolo wail, three times, then a pause. Again the loons called back to her, this time not stopping, as if the conductor of the orchestra had begun the concert. From every bay and island on Lac La Croix the loons began to sing, filling the air with their joyous, sorrowful, mysterious sound.

"Wow," Rachel whispered loudly when the singing had quieted. "That was better than surround sound, and I got it on tape."

"Shhhh," Hank cautioned, "we're coming up on the narrows where Danny and I swamped. We should be okay if we stay to the right. Danny, you follow at about twenty feet and listen for any directions we call out."

Silently, in the darkness of the narrows, the two canoes glided, one behind the other until they had passed the danger of the belly-ripping rocks and moved into deeper waters. Danny kept the Old Town about twenty feet to the right and a little behind his parents in the Seliga, carefully matching their paddling speed stroke for stroke. As he watched the dip-swing of their paddles in unison, it occurred to him that he seldom saw them spending time together these days. In fact, in the past year he had come to view them as such different and separate people that sometimes he wondered how they had ever found each other.

Maddy had grown up as the oldest child of four in a close-knit family. Her father was a famous heart-surgeon. Her mother had been his chief surgical nurse until they had their first child and she stayed home to raise the children. They were warm and generous grandparents, always welcoming. Family gatherings were loud, chaotic events with aunts and uncles talking above each other, cousins chasing around and plenty of delicious food.

Hank's parents had both died before Danny was born. There were no brothers or sisters, aunts, uncles or cousins— just Hank—and a kind of dark emptiness where his family might have fit in. At Maddy's family gatherings he would sometimes join in the festivities or sometimes stay by himself. In the past year, though, he had started skipping family get-togethers. Danny thought about his father's affection for Robert Service's poem "The Men That Don't Fit In." He wondered if this was how he felt around his mother's family?

Maddy had grown up in a prominent Minneapolis family, surrounded by a world of community, school, church, friends and relatives. Hank had grown up in near isolation in the Canadian wilderness, the adopted son and only child of a log cabin carpenter and a rural schoolteacher. It was his mother who had taught him the Ojibwe legends and respect for the First Peoples. It was his father who had taken him camping all throughout the lake region of northwestern Ontario, and taught him a respect for the power and beauty of nature.

Danny looked again at his parents paddling effortlessly across the water. Once again he was struck by the whiteness of his mother—her white-blond hair reflecting the silver moonlight. Tall, thin, fair-skinned, gentle, she reminded him of a doe in the woods, watching out for her young—vigilant. Her mind always ran clear, like the waters of Lac La Croix— smart, organized, self-assured. She was the stabilizing force in the family—calm, patient, understanding.

His father was the bear—dark and moody, but unpredictably playful. One day he might drop everything and lead Danny and Rachel out into the snow to spend an afternoon building a castle, complete with a snow-sculptured dragon, laughing at the fun of it until he cried with frozen fingers. At other times he would hole up for days in his painting studio, sleeping there on his dusty couch, his mind muddled with ideas, his mood depressed, troubled. Across the black water the darkness of his silhouette matched the darkness of the pine shadows. No moonlight could find him.

Danny wondered again how these two opposites had managed to find each other. Then he recalled hearing them talk about the magic of their first summer together at the canoeing camp where they had worked twenty-five years ago. They had taken an overnight canoe trip to Chance Lake on a day off together. Perhaps the power and beauty of nature had worked its magic on them—a night just like this beneath the stars—the surround sound of loons—the feel of the cool night breeze against their faces?

> *Hey-ho, anybody home*
> *Meat nor drink nor money have we none*
> *Still we will be merry*
> *Hey-ho anybody home*

Maddy began the singing again as she and Hank led the group northward, guided by the Polar Star. For nearly an hour they carefully navigated through a network of islands until finally they came to the open lake. Here, at a narrows between the American mainland and a fat island, the canoeists pulled up in a shallow bay to rest a spell before the big crossing.

Hank stepped into the water, calf-deep. "How's everyone doing?" He held both canoes steady in the water.

"I'm cold, and my butt's wet," Rachel complained. This was the duffer's dilemma. The water in the canoe from the wet boots would sometimes run under the duffer's seat; and because she wasn't paddling, Rachel's body was not warmed with the exercise.

"Here, put this on." Hank pulled off his sweatshirt and handed it to Rachel. He would paddle wearing just a T-shirt underneath his life jacket.

"How are you feeling, Bill?" Maddy turned in her seat to check on her patient.

"I feel okay. How much farther is it to the ranger station?"

Hank answered. "It's about three miles from this little bay to the ranger station, all open water." He handed pieces of licorice and hard candy to everyone except Bill. "It shouldn't take us much more than an hour." The white moon sat high in the southern sky behind them.

"What a beautiful night," Anne Tucker spoke softly. "I don't know if I'll ever return, but this sure is one beautiful night."

"How are you two doing?" Hank looked at Julie and Danny.

"I'm fine," said Julie. "This night paddling is kind of fun."

"Yeah, I know what you mean." Danny bit off another piece of licorice. "I'm okay," he told his dad.

"All right, campers, let's do it." Hank climbed back into the stern of the Seliga. "Stay together, now."

Lac La Croix—Lake of the Cross—crossing Lac La Croix—belly against belly—the widest stretch of open water in all of the Boundary Waters and Quetico—America on one side—Canada on the other—one wilderness—Danny felt at once puny and in awe of the magnificent lake. Three miles of open water up against two seventeen-foot wood canoes, one stroke at a time, slowly and in unison they paddled, not feeling the south wind until they were nearly halfway across. Then, with the first sliver of morning light along the eastern horizon, the wind decided to get a jump on the day. The big water began to rise and fall, awakening from its deep sleep, not quite making waves, more like undulations, pushing the canoes forward.

First Maddy, then Hank glanced over at the rookies,

checking their position. In the haze of the early dawn, they could just make out the tree line to the north.

"Welcome to Canada," Hank called out to his guests.

Danny figured that they must have crossed the border according to Hank's map calculations. Just a mile and a half of open water to go, straight ahead. He searched the faint horizon for the red maple leaf on the white background of the Canadian flag marking the location of the ranger station. Just then a big wave hit with a surge, pushing them forward like a surfboard. Waves increase in size the farther they are pushed across a lake, so as they got closer and closer to the north shore the waves from the south grew larger and larger. All experienced canoeists understood this—that paddling with the wind sometimes turned into surfing. Danny ruddered hard and began to enjoy the ride, pushed forward by the power of the wind and water, until nearer to shore where the waves began to break. "Whoa!" he cried out.

Hank looked over. "Follow us! Paddle harder now." He aimed the Seliga toward a small, sheltered bay. Danny looked up and saw the red maple leaf flapping in the wind above the trees directly in line with his father's canoe. Julie dug hard with her paddle. It was not a good time to switch sides. Giant wave after giant wave broke beneath the canoes, carrying them recklessly forward toward the rocky shoreline.

Just as Hank and Maddy reached the mouth of the bay, a lone fisherman in an open motorboat came around the point protecting the bay. Maddy waved and yelled at him. "Go get the ranger! It's an emergency!" They knew the ranger station would not be open this early. The ranger probably lived in a home on the First Nation community, not right at the ranger station. The fisherman nodded his head and motored off toward the west. All that was left for the rescuers was to cruise into the bay where the big waves broke apart and lost their energy.

"We did it!" Julie exclaimed as they rested their paddles and drifted up to the long wooden dock at the ranger cabin. The sky had lightened to a pale blue.

"Get me out of here. I hate duffing." Rachel reached for her father.

Hank was already wading knee-deep in the shallow water. He lifted Rachel out of the Old Town and stood her up on the dock. "Walk around to warm up. We'll make some hot cocoa in a few minutes." Then he turned to Anne and Bill Tucker. "Are you two dry?"

"Yes, thank you. That was quite a ride." Anne stood up stiffly as Maddy steadied the Seliga. Hank took her in his arms and swung her over onto the dock without getting her wet.

"Bill, are you ready?" Bill nodded his head and wiggled himself out from underneath the yoke, sitting up. Hank took him under his arms and Maddy took his legs. Together they lifted the big man onto the dock. He looked pale again. "I got the canoe," Hank said to Maddy, "better tend to your patient." Maddy climbed up onto the dock, kneeling down next to Bill.

By now, Danny and Julie had unloaded their packs and were lifting the Old Town up onto the wide dock. Then Danny helped Hank with the Seliga. Just as they set the Seliga down, a pickup truck pulled up next to the ranger cabin. A young Ojibwe woman in a ranger uniform came running down the path to the dock. She carried a big orange first aid kit.

"I'm the ranger in charge here." The Canadian flag flapped in the wind overhead. "What's the emergency?" Then she seemed to ignore everyone else and looked, almost startled, just at Hank Forester, as if she recognized him.

Maddy stepped forward. "I'm Dr. Madeline Forester. I'm an E.R. doctor. This man, Bill Tucker, may have had a heart attack nearly two days ago. We've been windbound. We need to get him to a hospital, now. This is Anne Tucker, his wife, and their daughter, Julie. They're from Ohio, in the States." In her green cotton hospital scrubs, Maddy Forester even looked like an E.R. doctor.

The young ranger immediately comprehended the gravity of the situation. "I'll call for an air ambulance. Use whatever you need in here." She set the first aid kit down on the dock, turned and ran back up the path to the ranger cabin.

It was five o'clock in the morning. Maddy stood with her arm around Rachel. Bill lay quietly, his head resting on a life jacket. Anne hugged Julie. Hank dug in the food pack for the cook stove and packets of cocoa. Danny looked back out over the lake with a feeling of gratitude. Missepishu had let them pass.

.   .   .

Just like Hank had described it, in half an hour a big orange helicopter appeared from the north and noisily dropped down right next to the dock, blowing the life jackets around. Floating on the water, its rubber pontoons bobbed up and down as its huge blades rotated slowly overhead. Two paramedics carrying a stretcher scrambled out of the air ambulance and onto the dock. Danny watched as Maddy took them aside for a moment, out of earshot of the Tuckers. Then the paramedics, an older man and a younger woman, strapped Bill onto the stretcher and slid him into the chopper. There would be room enough, too, for Anne, Julie and their one remaining pack. Rachel produced her camera and took pictures of everyone.

"Don't forget Bill's paddle." Hank handed it to Anne.

"How can we ever thank you enough?" Her eyes were filled with tears. She hugged Maddy. They had exchanged telephone numbers and addresses. Then Anne hugged Rachel. Finally she hugged Danny. "I want you to come visit us." She tousled his hair. Danny smiled and shrugged his shoulders.

Julie hugged Maddy and Rachel, too. But when she came to Danny, she paused, standing directly in front of him.

"I like your wood canoe," she said.

"I like your strong paddling." He reached out his hand to shake her hand. But instead of shaking his hand, Julie moved closer and gave him a big hug with a quick kiss on the cheek. Danny could feel his face turn red. But instead of turning away, he faced Julie Tucker, took his red ten-in-one compass device out of his pocket and handed it to her. "Here, this will help you find your way back to the Boundary Waters."

"Thank you," she said. Then his beautiful new friend turned and climbed into the helicopter with her parents. In less than a minute, they were up and away, disappearing over the tree line to the north.

chapter six

TWIN FALLS

After the sound of the helicopter had faded to the
north, the Foresters all followed the ranger up the
gravel path to the Quetico Park ranger station. Inside the log
structure they crowded around her work counter. Her
nametag read, "Renee Ruisseau." She pulled out her permit
booklet and spoke directly to Hank. "Were you planning on
entering the park?" she asked, sounding now more like a government official.

"We thought we'd try a two-night loop through Dark and
Argo Lakes, then back around to Curtain Falls." Hank
explained the route.

"The Dark River has no water in it. You'll never get
through to Dark Lake in this drought."

"What other choices do we have?"

"Where did you plan to camp tonight?"

"Right at Twin Falls." Hank and the ranger talked without
looking at a map.

"Then you could still travel south through Minn and McAree Lakes to Rebecca Falls. That route would take you back to Iron Lake and Curtain Falls."

Hank turned to Maddy. "What about it?"

"Sounds good to me. Just remember we have two very tired kids here. We've been up all night." Maddy put her arms around Danny and Rachel's shoulders. "How far of a paddle is it to Twin Falls?" She looked at Ranger Ruisseau.

"About nine miles."

"Well, it's only seven in the morning." Hank estimated the travel time in his head. "We could easily get there by noon and have half a layover day."

"Except for one thing." The ranger looked again at Hank, in earnest. "I forbid you to go out on the lake again in this wind. We had a drowning here, just two days ago. Four canoes headed out into big waves. One of them swamped. A fifty-year-old man drowned. He wasn't wearing his life preserver."

Hank looked at Maddy, then back to the serious young park ranger. "So what are we supposed to do? How are we supposed to get to the park?"

"I can call for a tow. I can call John Waterman. He has a boat for hauling canoes. He can come over from the community and give you a tow to Twin Falls."

Danny thought about his father's distaste for motorboats in the Boundary Waters. He imagined Hank bolting for the canoes and attempting some wild race against the Canadian officials. But technically, they were no longer in the Boundary Waters and had not yet entered the Quetico Provincial Park. They were on a Canadian Indian reserve, the Lac La Croix First Nation, with a very single-minded young park ranger calling the shots.

Maddy spoke up, sounding tired but smiling warmly at the ranger. "We very much appreciate your concern for our safety. After what we've been through in the last forty-eight hours, a tow from John Waterman sounds like a great idea."

"Yes!" Rachel pumped her little fist. "No more paddling in the wind for me."

"How much will this cost us?" Hank asked.

"I don't know. I'll call right now if that's what you want."

"Yes, that's what we want. A big motorboat ride in the middle of our pristine wilderness canoe trip." Hank shook his head. Danny could see that his father was smiling, though, sounding more relieved than sarcastic.

Ranger Ruisseau turned to a phone on the wall and dialed a number. She talked with her back to the Foresters. Then she turned back around, talking again to Hank. "John Waterman says ninety-four dollars American for a tow to Twin Falls. He can be here by about ten. First he has to fix a part on his outboard motor."

"It's a deal." Hank turned to Maddy. "I hope you have some cash."

Ranger Ruisseau hung up the phone. But before she wrote out a Quetico Park camping permit for the Foresters, she asked if they had obtained a Remote Area Border Crossing permit from Canadian Customs. Hank handed her the permit. She studied it, then looked up at Hank. "I see you are a Canadian citizen. From whereabouts?"

"I grew up near White Otter Lake, here in Ontario."

Hank Forester was part Native American, maybe a fourth-blood or more, but he didn't know from which tribal band he descended because he had been adopted by white parents. When he was eighteen, his family home, a log cabin near White Otter Lake, burned down. The fire destroyed nearly everything, including his adoption papers. His parents were never able to give him any specific information about his tribal heritage. His mother had understood he was Ojibwe, but there were over eighty Ojibwe bands in Ontario alone, so he never knew which exact Ojibwe band he might belong to. Hank had told this story to Danny as they sharpened their Hudson Bay camping axe before the trip. He explained that by returning to canoe country each year he felt at least some sense of connection with his family roots—both white and Native American.

Again, the young woman seemed to almost stare at Hank, but caught herself and finished filling out the park permit. Just like at the U.S. Forest Service ranger station, she reviewed the park rules with Danny and Rachel. "I see you have a stove. We, too, have a partial fire ban. So remember, no open fires in the morning, only between six o'clock and ten at night. Please be careful. The fire danger is extremely high right now." Everyone nodded.

"What about the Crane Lake fire?" Hank asked.

Ranger Ruisseau glanced out the window and then back at the Foresters. "The day before yesterday it blew up, jumped the firebreak to the north and overran one of the fire crews. Six American firefighters had to crawl into their fire shelters... their shake 'n' bakes. That's when the Americans asked us for help with our water bombers."

"Oh, no!" Maddy gasped. "Our older son, Mike, is a fire-fighter on the American side." Rachel put her arm around her mother's waist. "What else do you know? Was anyone hurt... burned?"

Ranger Ruisseau shook her head. "That's all I know. The fire is under control now, mostly just clean up work, hot spots and such. Good thing for us that the wind didn't turn west, or we'd all be looking for shelter."

Maddy pressed on. "Can you find out more about the firefighters? Call park headquarters or something?"

"I'll see what I can do." The young ranger seemed sympathetic to Maddy's concern for Mike.

Maddy paid the park fee and purchased a small booklet

about the park's pictographs and Quetico T-shirts for herself and Rachel. Danny had brought along his park sweatshirt from last year's trip. Hank added an Ontario fishing license to the purchases, and they were set to explore the Quetico.

Just as the Minnesota family was leaving the building, Ranger Ruisseau asked one more question. "Have you folks eaten any breakfast?"

Maddy answered. "Not really, but we'll be okay. We have some trail lunch we can eat… trail lunch and orange drink and cocoa."

Ranger Ruisseau nodded.

·　·　·

Back down on the dock the south wind had already picked up speed. Giant waves pushed deeper and deeper into the sheltered bay. Treetops swayed back and forth, at times cracking overhead. Danny could see the wisdom of the ranger's suggestion for a tow. Wind was the great friend of campers during mosquito season, but the great enemy on the water. Three days of sun and wind had beaten down hard on the Foresters. Their energy was spent, like waves dying in the shallows. No one had the will to prepare a breakfast. So they just sat together on the dock with their backs resting against the Old Town, desiring only sleep.

But Maddy couldn't sleep. "Hank," she announced, looking out over the lake, "this trip is over."

"What?!" Hank asked.

"Tell John Waterman to tow us back to the portage to the Moose River. We can be back at the Echo Trail landing by nightfall, drive into Ely and check on Mike."

"I will not do that." Hank sounded irritated by Maddy's demand. "There is no reason to quit this trip. I have every confidence in Mike. He's a survivor, a fighter."

The fight was on. "He's an impulsive nineteen-year-old, not unlike his father." Maddy's voice tightened. "Well, you can stay out here in this fire trap, but my daughter and my younger son and I will be sleeping in the Hotel Ely tonight, if not sitting around some hospital waiting room."

"Wait a minute," Danny cut into the fight, "don't you remember what Mike said about trying to meet up with us on Iron Lake? What if we're not there and he shows up? Wouldn't he be as worried about us as we are about him?"

"Good point," Maddy conceded. "If only I could be sure he was safe."

"Look, we're all pretty wrung out from this ordeal with the Tuckers." Hank tried to reason with Maddy. "Let's just give it a rest, regroup, and talk about it when our tow arrives."

"You're right." Maddy stood up. "I need to get out of the sun. Come on, Rachel, we can take a nap under the canoe." Maddy and Rachel made beds for themselves lying head to head on sleeping pads in the shade beneath the Old Town. Soon, mother and daughter were asleep in the morning wind. Ranger Ruisseau didn't seem to mind. Perhaps she knew that no other canoeists would be arriving that day. Only the Foresters had crossed deadly Lac La Croix that night.

For another hour, Danny and Hank passed the time skipping flat stones from off the beach, chewing on pieces of licorice all the while. "Sixteen skips... that's your best yet in these waves." Danny counted for his father. Then, for a while, they just sat on the dock and watched the waves wash up on the shoreline.

· · ·

Right at ten o'clock John Waterman rounded the point in his big blue powerboat, making his way toward the dock. At about a hundred feet out he cut back on the power and maneuvered his vessel into the dock. Danny could see that he had a boy with him, just about his age. The boy threw a bowline to Hank and a stern rope to Danny. They pulled the powerboat alongside the dock and secured the ropes to big metal cleats. Maddy and Rachel had already awakened from their nap and walked up to the ranger cabin to ask Ranger Ruisseau if she had heard anything about the Crane Lake fire-fighters or Bill Tucker.

John Waterman ducked out from under the canopy of his boat and stepped onto the dock without really looking at Hank or Danny. "Wood canoes," was the first thing he said. "We'll be careful not to scratch the gunwales." He pointed to the padded canoe rack on top of his boat. "This is my son, Troy." He motioned to the lanky, sun-tanned boy with a black shock of hair. Troy joined his father on the dock with a nod of his head to Danny, but like the ranger, his eyes locked onto Hank Forester.

Quickly, though, Hank, Danny, John Waterman and his son set about lifting the canoes up onto the steel rack and tightly strapping them down. Danny and Troy loaded the paddles, cook kit and tent. Hank and John Waterman loaded the three packs. By the time Maddy and Rachel returned from the ranger cabin, all that was left for them to do was to put on their life jackets and step into the boat. "No news about the Tuckers," Maddy reported as she lifted Rachel up onto the deck and climbed aboard herself. "But the ranger says all the American firefighters got out safely... no one burned or hos-pitalized." She smiled slightly and shook her head. "Lucky Mike. Let's hope he finds us camped on Iron Lake."

Lucky Mike, Danny thought to himself as he and his father cast off the bow and stern lines and jumped onto the boat. *Luck and skill.*

There was plenty of room for passengers on the two

bench seats facing each other in the hold of the boat. Hank and Danny sat on one side, Maddy and Rachel on the other. Troy Waterman sat behind his father facing the Foresters. The boatsman revved up the big 125 horsepower Mercury engine and pointed his ferry into the waves.

"John and Troy," Hank shouted above the loud outboard, "this is my wife, Maddy, and our daughter, Rachel." Hank had already paid for the tow with cash.

John Waterman nodded politely, glancing over his shoulder at the women. He was wearing a blue baseball cap. Then he shifted into high gear and the hull of his boat began slamming against the big waves, one after another, as they left the relative shelter of the bay for the open waters of Lac La Croix. Danny held onto the railing, glad he was not attempting to paddle in these rough waves.

Troy Waterman smiled a friendly smile at the Foresters. Then he handed a birchbark basket to Maddy. It was covered with a blue and white checkered napkin. Maddy lifted the cloth and smiled. "Thank you." She smiled even more broadly at the young man, then showed the contents of the basket to her family. "Breakfast," she announced. The basket was filled with blueberry muffins, oranges and little cartons of milk. Everyone grabbed a muffin.

"My mother thought you might like some of her freshly-baked muffins." Troy explained.

"How old are you?" Maddy asked him as she peeled an orange.

"Thirteen."

"Hey, same as me." Danny gave a thumbs-up sign.

"Do you have a little sister?" Rachel asked.

"Yeah, her name is Christy, but we call her bird-girl."

The Foresters all laughed.

"That's what we call her." Danny pointed to his little sister.

"Why do you call her bird-girl?" Rachel wanted to know.

"My dad's a wildlife photographer. He mostly photographs bald eagles and ospreys in the Quetico. Christy likes to help him find eagle nests. That's why we call her bird-girl. I'd rather go fishing than chase eagles." Troy looked to the front of the boat, and then back at the Foresters. "Once in a while, if the ranger calls us, we tow windbound tourists over to the park."

The word *tourists* stung a bit for Danny to hear. That was a word his father used to describe inexperienced campers. It never occurred to him that someone else would think of them as *tourists*. He looked across the lake in the direction the boat was traveling.

Out on the open water the waves crested higher and higher.

"What if I get seasick?" Rachel asked her mother.

"Then just puke over the side," she said.

Knowing the wilderness region like the Foresters knew their neighborhood, John Waterman navigated eastward without a map, lake water spraying up on the windshield of his boat. The canoes sat overhead like a double-arched cedar roof. Hank Forester stared straight ahead, too, looking over John Waterman's right shoulder. It was too loud for conversation. But Danny wondered even if they could be heard, would anyone speak what they all must be thinking—that, astonishingly, John Waterman could pass as the identical twin brother to Hank Forester, and vice versa. Danny looked across at Maddy and Rachel, raising his eyebrows. They looked back at him, raising their eyebrows, all certain of this one thought—the uncanny, amazing resemblance between these two men. Danny wondered if Troy Waterman recognized the similarities between their fathers.

"Can we show them the moose?" Troy Waterman shouted over his shoulder to his father. John Waterman nodded his head. Then Troy pointed to a big island up ahead. John turned sharply into a shallow bay and cut back on the power. There, standing in the marsh grass along the shoreline, a bull moose lifted his huge rack toward the sound of the boat. "We always see him in this bay." Troy smiled. Rachel took a picture. John Waterman revved his engine twice and the massive animal bolted for the trees.

Back on course, the Foresters sat without talking, scanning the rugged landscape. On their left, to the north, the reservation land stretched for miles. On their right, to the south, the vastness of Lac La Croix spread out toward the U.S. Straight ahead, eastward, Bell Island created two rocky narrows around itself, both leading to Twin Falls where the Maligne River poured into Lac La Croix and the campers would enter the Quetico Park. John Waterman chose the north channel and slowed to half-speed. The sound of the falls could be heard in the distance. In a few minutes, rounding a bend in the narrows, magnificent Twin Falls appeared—two tumbling waterfalls split around a black rock, tree-covered island. A wet mist lifted up from the white rumbling water and drifted toward the boat as the group approached the landing at the portage.

The boatsman slowed in the current and maneuvered into shore. Hank stepped up on the deck and jumped down onto the rocks, rope in hand. He gently pulled the craft into shore, careful of the hull on the rocks. Then as quickly as they had loaded their canoes and gear, they unloaded everything onto land again. "Thank you! Thank you!" The Foresters waved to their guides as John Waterman let his boat drift back out into the current before starting the engine.

"There's a bear-pole up in the campsite," he shouted over the roar of the falls, pointing up to the campsite beside the rumbling whitewater. "You better hang your pack tonight." Then he started his engine, caught the fast moving current and disappeared around the bend. Troy Waterman waved from the rear of the boat. Danny understood that to an outdoorsman like John Waterman and his family, the Foresters must look like the rookies—the *tourists*. He wondered what it would be like to live Troy Waterman's life, so close to the wilderness.

. . .

The path from the landing to the campsite was a short but steep climb. Rachel ran ahead, carrying nothing but her waterproof camera and the cook kit.

"Rachel, I don't want you going near the falls without your father or me beside you." Maddy chased after her, tent in hand.

This left the grunt work for the men. Hank flipped up the

Old Town. Danny grabbed the food pack. Together they made three trips up and back and up again to the damp, rocky campsite. There was barely one decent tent site, and no fire grate, just a fire pit. Unlike the Boundary Waters Canoe Area Wilderness, in the Quetico Park there were no fire grates or biffies at the campsites. The Canadians liked to rough it.

Firewood was scarce. Danny could see that this was one of those overused campsites where the vegetation had been trampled and stripped bare in places. He hated to see this. "Do we have to stay right here?" he asked his parents as they sat on some logs around the fire pit, snacking on some of Maddy's voyageur bars. "There's still plenty of daylight left for us to find another campsite."

Maddy spoke. "Danny, we're all so tired. I think we should just stay here tonight. We can cook something quick on the camp stove. At six we can start a small fire and burn our garbage. You and Hank can hang the food pack. Then we can all hit the sack for a long summer's nap. Maybe tomorrow we can have a normal day on the trail, like we were supposed to have on this trip."

"I agree." Hank supported Maddy's plan.

"What about fishing? We've hardly done any fishing," Danny complained to his father.

"Danny, it's been too windy. Besides, I just don't feel like fishing tonight. If this is bear territory, I don't want to leave fish guts around, even buried, and there's not enough firewood for a good fish-gut fire."

"Oh, no! How are we going to hear a bear in the night beneath the sound of the waterfalls?" Rachel looked worried.

"That's why we're going to hang the food pack and why no little girls are going to bring candy into the tent." Maddy tousled her hair.

Danny accepted his parents' decision. He decided the campsite wasn't so bad after all. It had a terrific view of the falls and it was protected from the wind. In the morning, he could go fishing. For now, he would help Rachel pitch the tent and scrounge up as much dry firewood as they could find back in the woods. Later, he promised himself, when his father was out of earshot, he would ask his mother and sister about what they thought about the John Waterman—Hank Forester lookalike phenomenon. He was afraid to ask his dad.

Maddy crawled into the pitched tent just as Danny and Rachel finished laying out the sleeping bags and pads. It was the first time in three days that Danny had even seen the inside of the tent. There was more work to do outside, but the three exhausted campers fell onto the soft bedding, moaning with relief for their tired bodies. And even though it was only noon on the fourth day of their trip, a massive fatigue set into their bones and they fell instantly into a deep wilderness sleep. No dreams for Danny.

Six hours later, Hank woke his slumbering family. He had made quick work of dinner—a freeze-dried, add-boiling-water meal of beef stroganoff, with instant cherry cobbler for desert. They had planned a couple of these easy meals for just this sort of situation, using the one-burner camp stove. Not every campsite would allow time and firewood for baking bread.

After dinner, Danny found the bear-pole on his search for firewood. About fifty feet into the woods, away from the fire pit, someone had taken the effort to raise a long red pine pole twenty feet above the ground and lash it horizontally between two thin white pines. The white pines stood about ten feet apart. All the Foresters had to do was throw a rope over the center of the pole and hoist their food pack into the air. Hank made sure their food was safely packed away, except for one bottle of bug juice and some popcorn they could finish off before bedtime.

He tied a rock to one end of his bear rope. "Watch out!"

he called out as he threw the rock and rope up and over the pole. The rock came swinging back at him, but he stepped aside and caught the rope. "Pull hard, now." Hank had Rachel helping him. Danny and his mother watched. The idea was to hang the food pack out of reach to any bear from the ground, from the pole across the top and from either pine tree. "Good job." Hank secured the rope to a third tree. He looked tired. It had been a very long day.

Back at the fire pit Danny and Rachel built a small campfire. Hank had fetched a pot of water to heat for cleaning dishes. With their work complete, the Foresters four sat down on the ridge above the falls. A red August sun angled low in the western sky, reflecting light off the mist below them, creating prisms of color here and there over the water. They drank the last of the orange bug juice and passed a pan of popcorn between them.

"What if a bear comes into our campsite tonight? I don't know if I can go back to sleep." Rachel was still worried about bears.

"I used to be afraid of bears, but on last year's trip I got over that." Danny tried to reassure his little sister. "A bear doesn't want any more to do with you than you want to do with it."

"But what if...?" Rachel continued. But just then the mosquitoes hit. Swarms of mosquitoes arising at dusk.

"Head for the tent," Maddy called out. Everyone scrambled to their feet.

"You guys go ahead. I'll get the fire." Hank made sure all the food scraps and garbage had been burned. Then he quickly doused the fire. In a minute, he was at the tent door, swatting away the huge Canadian mosquitoes. "Let me in!"

"Quick!" Maddy unzipped the door. "Don't let any mosquitoes in."

Hank tumbled, stocking-footed, into the tent. They all left

their campsite shoes just outside the tent door. Inside the tent, everyone found his or her place. Hank lay down next to one side, with Maddy next to him, then Rachel, with Danny next to the other wall of the tent.

"Whew! That was close," said Hank. "We could have been carried away and eaten alive." Mosquitoes buzzed all around the tent.

"Don't tease, Hank," Maddy chided him quietly. "Rachel's scared enough of bears."

But Rachel, who had worried about being able to fall asleep, had crawled into her sleeping bag and again instantly fallen asleep.

Danny also felt the heaviness of sleep bear down upon him. He lay quietly on his back, hands behind his head with his eyes closed. Lying there, as the sun set, he reviewed in his mind the remarkable events of the last three days—sighting the Crane Lake fire from Warrior Hill—the mysterious feeling at the pictograph cliffs—rescuing the Tuckers—swamping with his father—paddling at night—the big orange helicopter. He thought, too, about the amazing resemblance between John Waterman and his father, "The Men That Don't Fit In" and the sad emptiness in Hank Forester's life where a family might have stood. But mostly, before drifting off to sleep beneath the steady roar of Twin Falls, Danny Forester thought about the beautiful and talented Julie Tucker from Ohio, and the feel of her soft warm lips pressed against his right cheek.

chapter seven

BEAVER LODGE

B eneath the rushing sound of the falls, Danny was awakened by the sound of little animal feet scampering across the tent. Mice? Chipmunks? Sunlight cast shadows of branches across the nylon tent fabric—still branches. Had the wind finally quit? He scanned the inside of the tent. Rachel lay sound asleep, snuggled up next to her mother, also sound asleep. Hank's sleeping bag lay empty. Danny guessed he was already out fishing.

He found his father standing alongside the rapids below the falls casting for bass. He had set up Danny's rig with a glow-in-the-dark lure and popped open the collapsible fishing net. "Out there." Hank plopped a red plastic leech about forty feet out into the current. Danny picked up his rod and reel and tried his first cast. Catch and release—they were using hooks without barbs. "I've already released four... nice ones."

"Any walleyes?" Danny asked.

"No, all smallies."

For more than two hours father and son fished beneath the morning sun, talking little, lost in a current of time, lost in a stream of smallmouth bass—caught and released, caught and released, one after another—just for the sheer joy of it.

"Hey, how about some help with breakfast?" Maddy called from the campsite above them. She and Rachel had slept for nearly twelve hours.

"Be right there," Hank responded, casting his leech a final time.

Back up in the campsite, Danny helped his father lower the food pack from the bear pole. "Have you talked to Mom about me doing a solo?" he asked as he held the pack for Hank to untie the rope.

"We're thinking about it." Hank worked on a knot without looking up. "That's the best answer I can give you for now. Why don't you go get the fishing poles while I cook breakfast."

At least the answer wasn't "no," Danny thought to himself. He hustled back down to the rapids to gather up their fishing gear. Maddy and Rachel were packing up the personal packs inside the tent. Fifteen minutes later they all met at the fire pit where Hank had cooked a pot of cereal over the one-burner camp stove.

"What's this?" Rachel looked at the gooey white blob Hank had plopped with a spoon into her sierra cup.

"Rice and raisins." Hank smiled. "Put some cinnamon and sugar on it. You'll like it."

"I thought we voted this down," Danny complained.

"You can never vote down rice and raisins." Hank stuck a big spoonful into his mouth.

"Mmmm...Mmmm." Maddy smiled and dug in with her spoon, too. "We gotta' have rice and raisins or it's not a Forester canoe trip." Danny and Rachel rolled their eyes at each other, but ate their portions hurriedly, washing the sticky cereal down with gulps of freeze-dried orange juice.

"Where're we going today?" Rachel wanted to know.

Hank spread a new map out on the ground. "We'll head back south, into Minn Lake, maybe McAree Lake for tonight. We were going to loop through Dark Lake, where there are some great palisades and pictographs, and then into Argo, a really beautiful lake, but the ranger says the Dark River has no water in it, so we can't get through." Hank pointed to their route on the map. A narrow stretch of water led from the Maligne River to the eastern end of a long, finger-like Lac La Croix bay called Martin Bay. Three small portages were marked along the narrow stretch as nine-rods, thirteen-rods and six-rods long. A ninety-rod portage led from Martin Bay to Minn Lake.

"Those don't look too bad." Rachel had learned to read the map.

"We'll see," said Hank, "we'll see."

The rested travelers broke camp in short order and loaded their wood canoes in the clear waters of the broad Maligne River above Twin Falls. Then, under a brilliant blue sky, they paddled east a short stretch upstream before turning south into the narrows leading to Martin Bay and Minn Lake. Here the water was low, and three short portages would turn into seven muddy and frustrating portages. So, it was nearly noon when the Foresters came upon an expansive beaver pond surrounded by aspen trees. Before them stood the most massive beaver dam and beaver lodge any of them had ever seen.

"This must be the center of all beaverdom." Danny marveled at the enormity of the beaver structures as they paddled across the pond. The beaver dam itself stood at least six feet above the water line and stretched over sixty yards long from one end to the other. The lodge stood at least eight feet out of the water and spread out maybe forty feet across its base. Grass was growing on top if it.

"This must be where the emperor beaver lives. All the other beaver lodges I've ever seen are just little beaver outposts, and all the other beavers I've ever seen have just been ambassador beavers sent out from this spot by the emperor beaver." Hank joined in with his imagination. "I've never seen anything like this."

"Yikes! What if it's the lost world of one of those six-foot prehistoric beavers?" Rachel carried the story a step further.

Hank maneuvered the red canoe alongside the huge beaver house. He and Rachel scrambled up on top of the massive pile of sticks and mud. Danny and his mother followed in the green canoe. Maddy pulled a bottle of bug juice, the TL bag and some of her voyageur bars out of the food pack. On the grassy top of the ancient emperor beaver lodge, there was room enough for all four of them to sit down and eat their snack.

"I wonder how long the beavers have been working on this dam? Maybe hundreds of years?" Hank surveyed the beaver kingdom. "Look at the base of that dam, it must be twenty feet across. A whole civilization of beavers must have built this thing."

"It'd be cool to get inside this lodge. I wonder if there are any beavers in there now?" Rachel rapped on the top of the lodge with a stick. "Hello Mr. and Mrs. Beaver! Come out so I can take your picture."

"Don't be a nerd, Rachel," Danny chided her.

"Oh, you think you're so cool just because Julie Tucker kissed you."

"Shut up, brat!"

"Nahh... nahh... nahh... Julie Tucker kissed you."

"Time to go, campers." Hank lifted Rachel back into the bow of the Seliga for the short paddle from the lodge to the dam. Then they portaged over the dam and carried their canoes and gear downstream another fifty yards to find water deep enough to put in again. Eventually, they made their way through the narrows to Martin Bay. Danny paddled stern in the Old Town, with Maddy in the bow.

Skinny Martin Bay ran nearly six miles inland west to east from the main body of Lac La Croix. The Foresters would need to paddle only the last half mile or so due east before the ninety-rod portage to Minn Lake. They found the end of the shallow bay thick with lily pads, horsetail rushes and wild rice. Dark green painted turtles sunned themselves on floating logs, then dove into the water as the canoes approached. Purple dragonflies buzzed back and forth through the hot summer air. A mother merganser feigned injury and splashed her brood of ducklings away from the intruders. Then they all heard the boisterous canoeists before sighting them—a bad sign.

In a minute, a rowdy group of eight young men in four lightweight canoes came racing around a slight bend in Martin Bay. Yelling and laughing at each other, they soon overtook and passed the Foresters. Their canoes were piled high with packs and fishing gear, even ice chests. As the last canoe passed them, a scruffy-looking young man in the stern looked back with a sneer and said, "I bet we get the last campsite on Minn Lake." Then he mocked the Foresters with three lily-dips of his paddle before racing off again.

Danny heard a bear-like growl emanate from deep within his father's chest. Maddy turned in the bow and looked back at Hank. Their eyes met. Danny understood that a challenge had been laid down to the old camp team. His mother and father had once won a canoe race at camp; and today, a new race was on. He could sense the intensity even in Maddy's powerful bow strokes.

A few minutes later, they caught up with the group at the beginning of the portage into Minn Lake. The last of the men, who all looked about twenty years old, were heading down the trail into the woods with canoes on their shoulders. The shoreline was strewn with packs, ice chests and huge tackle boxes—even fish-finders. This told the Foresters that the challengers were planning to make two trips over the portage. But they would do it in one trip—this was how they planned to win.

Instead of taking his rucksack as usual with the Seliga,

Hank put the small pack on Rachel's back and handed her the cook kit. He spoke in a low tone with his hand on top of her pith helmet. "Rachel, we are going to teach these boys a lesson in portaging, and you're going to be part of the winning team. Now, I want you to stay with me. Walk as fast as you can. Okay?" Rachel nodded her head. Then Hank pulled the food pack out of the Old Town and hefted it onto his back. It was the first time Danny had ever seen his father carry a food pack. Hank was a canoe carrier, not a food pack carrier. But next, Danny witnessed something even more amazing. With the food pack on his back, Hank turned and flipped the red Seliga up onto his shoulders—on wounded legs he would double-pack with the food pack and canoe! "Follow me," he said to Rachel, and moosed out of the water with a grunt. Rachel tagged hurriedly after him.

Danny and his mother flipped the Old Town up onto her shoulders. "I'll catch up with them. Can you get the rest?" she asked, leaving Danny with the tent and the two personal packs.

"I got it."

"Okay, Dan-man," she said. "Let's show those guys what the Foresters are made of." Then she too stepped lively up the trail. The Old Town was lighter in weight than the Seliga, and the yoke pads were set for Maddy's shoulders. Both Hank and Maddy preferred to carry canoes rather than packs.

Danny was a bit surprised to see such a competitive spirit aroused in his mother, but he quickly flipped the larger pack, a #3 Duluth pack, onto his back. Then he pulled the smaller #2 Duluth pack across his chest. He threw the tent across the top of the pack on his back and headed up the portage—double-packed front and back. This way of double-packing made it hard to see the trail, but at least if he fell he would probably land on a pack and not get hurt.

About halfway across Danny began to meet up with the

first of the men coming back over the portage. He thought he caught a whiff of alcohol as the men passed him one by one, stepping aside for the kid with the packs. At least they had the courtesy to step aside, or perhaps Hank Forester had already given them some instructions in trail etiquette. Maybe it was just the guy in the stern of the last canoe who was behaving like a jerk. But it didn't matter now. Hank and Maddy had decided to teach them a lesson. After he passed the men, he heard one of them shout from behind him, "Go for it, kid!" They knew they had lost the race.

It wasn't an especially difficult hike, but Danny didn't catch up with his family until the end of the portage. Both canoes were floating in the water. Rachel was sitting in the bow of Hank's canoe. He had taken the food pack, too. Maddy stood knee-deep by the stern of the Old Town. Danny understood that she intended to paddle stern if there was going to be a race across Minn Lake to the last available campsite.

"Come on, come on," Maddy spoke in low tones, urging Danny to hurry. She lifted the packs off Danny's front and back and loaded them into the Old Town. They surveyed the scene for a moment. The rough-looking group of men had dumped their canoes and gear in a tangled mess at the portage landing. All eight of them had headed back for more equipment, most of which they didn't even need.

Hank just shook his head. "Tourists," he mumbled under his breath, "tourists." Then he stepped again into the stern of the red canoe. Danny and his mother followed in the Old Town. The winners paddled briskly out onto Minn Lake, not even looking back. A slight afternoon breeze came at them sideways from the west. The wind had changed. Perhaps a welcome rain would follow.

The young men were right. Four of the five campsites on Minn Lake were already occupied by other campers. This left the least desirable campsite for the Foresters, but it was good enough. The campsite sat on the eastern shore of the lake atop a steep rock face that sloped into the water like a smaller version of Warrior Hill. The only difficulty was hauling all the gear up to the campsite, but the campsite itself was flat and wide open, offering a great view of the lake. The breeze from the west kept the mosquitoes down. But best of all, someone had left a huge pile of firewood next to the fire pit.

"Who wants to help make trail pizza?" Maddy would cook.

"I do!" Rachel chimed in. It was approaching dinnertime and the window of opportunity to build a fire.

"Want help with the fire?" Hank offered.

"No, I think we can do it." Maddy smiled. "Besides, I want to see if I can still light a fire, and I can teach Rachel."

Hank groaned. This meant that he and Danny would have to take their turn at pitching the tent. Next to carrying the food pack, Hank hated pitching the tent. For no particular reason—he just didn't like to be bothered with it. Or maybe, as Danny thought, it was because his father really didn't like sleeping in tents. He remembered the story Hank had told him on last year's trip with Mike. When he was about Danny's age he had been camping with his own father. Hank had sneaked a chocolate bar with him into the tent. That night a black bear ripped open the side of the tent looking for that chocolate bar. Ever since then, if it weren't for mosquitoes or rain, Hank preferred to sleep under the stars.

"I can do the tent," Danny volunteered, sensing his father's reluctance.

"No, let's do it together," Hank grumbled and grabbed the tent bag.

Danny grumbled silently to himself, because he knew that with his father the tent would have to be pitched perfectly. This meant finding a tent site with a slight slope, clearing away every little sharp rock, stick and pinecone, and positioning the doorway just right into the wind. Of course, Danny would be the one down on his knees clearing away the rocks, sticks and pinecones. Hank took charge of tent stakes, axe in hand. He surveyed the campsite. "Over here." He chose a spot. Danny knew his job and squatted down. As he cleared away the debris for the tent site, he again noticed how dry the ground was—the duff held no moisture.

Twenty minutes later they worked at stringing a clothesline between the red pines for drying wet socks. "Hey, look at that." Hank pointed out over the lake. Maddy and Rachel came over from the fire pit. The four of them stood together where the edge of the trees met the top of the sloping rock face. They watched as the eight young men in their four lightweight canoes paddled south down the center of the lake, headed for the portage to McAree Lake and a late supper. No one waved. Hank finished tying the clothesline rope, then strung his hammock between two trees overlooking the lake.

Back at the fire pit, Maddy tended to a thick cheese pizza baking in the reflector oven. Rachel had mixed up two bottles of bug juice and set out plates, cups and silverware on the red-checkered tablecloth.

"Man, I'm hungry!" Hank eyed Maddy's delicious-looking pizza.

"Me, too." Danny looked for his plate.

"Let's gather around." Maddy led the grace as they held hands in a circle. "We are grateful…"

"…for a normal day on the trail with my family and no catastrophes." Danny thought for a moment about the Tuckers.

"…for all the birds and animals." Rachel had set her camera next to her plate, hoping for the appearance of the Whiskey Jacks.

"...for this chance to show my children my homeland." Hank reminded them that they were still in Canada.

"...for Mike's safety and this time with you." Maddy sounded almost tearful.

"Amen," they said together, and sat down around the fire to eat.

After supper Danny and Rachel washed dishes. Maddy reorganized the food pack, setting aside graham crackers, marshmallows and chocolate bars for s'mores. Hank made his way to the hammock and stretched out, his arms dangling from the sides. The sun had moved low in the western sky. A few moments later, Danny looked up from his dishwashing pot and saw that his mother had joined his father in the hammock. She had crawled in beside him, and Hank had wrapped his long arms around her. Together they swayed gently in the warm evening breeze. Danny nudged Rachel with his elbow and gave her the raised-eyebrow sign. She reached for her camera. It was the first time in a long time that Danny had seen such an expression of affection between his parents. He remembered the story about their honeymoon canoe trip and wondered if the northwoods had again worked its magic. Perhaps it was winning the race to the campsite that brought them together. Rachel snapped a picture and smiled at Danny, giving him the raised-eyebrow sign back. Then they reached for the bag of marshmallows.

"I'll get some sticks." Danny searched through the firewood pile and broke off four thin aspen branches. He took his Swiss army knife and sharpened each end. "Be careful, now." He handed one of the sticks to Rachel. "Don't run with that."

"I'll be careful." Rachel stuck two marshmallows onto the end of her stick. She held the white treats above the fire. Danny added a few more pieces of firewood and started to roast his own marshmallows. All of a sudden Rachel's marshmallows burst into flames. "Yikes!" She flipped her stick up out of the flames—but a little too hard. The flaming marsh-mallows let loose, flew through the air and landed in the dry pine needles on the ground behind her. Poof! Instantly the pine needles burst into flame. "Oh, no!"

Danny jumped up. "Mom! Dad!" He stomped on the spreading flames. Hank and Maddy flipped out of the ham-mock and landed with a thud on the ground, both looking up at the fire. "Grab the dishwater!" Danny yelled at Rachel, still stomping on the flames.

Screaming, Rachel grabbed the big pot of water and threw it toward the fire, but missed most of the spreading flames.

"Danny! Get some more water!" Hank yelled, grabbing the shovel.

Danny grabbed the big pot and two others and ran down the rock to the landing, Rachel screaming in fright behind him. Turning, muscles straining with pots full of water, he ran up hill again, astonished up on top to see red-yellow flames engulfing a small mountain maple bush.

"Hurry!" Hank yelled, grabbing one of the pots of water from Danny. Together, they poured water on the burning bush, while Maddy beat the flaming duff with a wet towel. The flames were dead but the dry ground around the moun-tain maple still smoldered. Smoke drifted across the campsite. Standing back, Danny was amazed to see how in a matter of seconds the fire had blackened a circle on the ground ten feet in diameter. *How could Mike enjoy facing something as frighten-ing as this,* he thought to himself, feeling shaky and breath-less.

"I'm sorry. I'm sorry," Rachel cried, trembling.

"It's okay, honey." Maddy hugged her. "It was an acci-dent."

"Let's get more water." Hank and Danny hauled water in the cook kit pots—five trips down and back from the lake to make sure the campfire and the marshmallow fire were total-ly extinguished.

"Man, that was scary," Danny poured his last pot of water on the campfire and stirred the ashes. "I didn't realize the dry duff could catch fire that fast." Hank made sure the spot where the marshmallow fire had erupted was completely soaked.

"I think it's time for bed," Maddy suggested when their fire prevention work was completed. The sun had just dropped below the tree line to the west and the wind had died down. A din of mosquito buzzing could be heard rising out of the forest behind them. Rachel was first into the tent. Everyone followed, quickly zipping the door shut. Each person found their place and made themselves comfortable, like a family of deer bedding down for the night.

As the sky darkened, Danny stared at the translucent ceiling of the tent, thinking about taking a solo—just one night alone at a campsite—to prove to himself he could do it. With only two nights left on the trip, would his parents let him try? He was afraid to ask again.

But Rachel wasn't much afraid to ask anything. "Dad," she talked in the dark.

"What's on your mind, fire-girl?"

"You know that guy who gave us the boat ride to Twin Falls?"

"Yes, I remember. His name was John Waterman. What about him?"

"Did you happen to notice that he looked an awful lot like you?"

"Rachel!" Danny jabbed her with his elbow.

"It's okay, Danny." Hank calmed him down. "To be honest, Rachel, I didn't really notice. Now, why don't you try to catch some shut-eye. We're all pretty tired and we have a long paddle down McAree Lake tomorrow."

"Okay, goodnight." Rachel accepted her father's answer.

Danny thought about this answer. *How could he not notice,* he wondered. But fatigue overtook him. Soon the first loon began its nightly calling, then another and another, creating a rhapsody of natural sound that carried Danny's mind into a dream world of images—pictographs and smallmouth bass, painted turtles and hooded mergansers, emperor beaver lodges and exploding marshmallows. Like a feather caught in a whirlpool, the images swirled in his mind until he fell into a deep, deep sleep.

chapter eight

TINDERBOX

By dawn the Foresters all lay awake, sweltering in their nylon tent. In the absence of wind, the lake had lost its nighttime cooling effect. The summer heat had already forced the mosquitoes back into the forest. The smell of Rachel's marshmallow fire hung in the air.

"We might as well get up and get an early start on the day." Maddy stretched her arms out. "Come on, Rachel, let's take a little hike into the woods."

One by one the campers crawled out of the stuffy tent and stood barefooted on the pine needle carpet of the campsite. Danny slipped on his sneakers and walked over to the edge of the rock slope to check out the lake—smooth as glass. There were no signs of activity at any of the other campsites. He sat down on a flat, bench-like rock. Hank followed, limping stiffly from his double-packing the day before. He sat down next to Danny, map in hand.

"Tell me what you had in mind for this solo idea of

yours." They looked over the next day's route. "After viewing Curtain Falls, we were planning to take the Stuart River south tomorrow, out of Iron Lake. But now I'm wondering if we can even get through there in this low water. It might be better for us to head back to Lac La Croix and up the Moose River."

Danny pointed to the southern area of Lac La Croix. "There." He put his finger on a place marked Bear Island. "That's what I was thinking... a solo on Bear Island." He waited for his father to respond, but their conversation was interrupted by Rachel's yammering.

"I don't know what's worse, those nasty biffies in the Boundary Waters or having to dig your own latrine in the Quetico? Yuck! Where're the towelettes?" She walked up behind them holding a roll of toilet paper.

Hank laughed. Maddy walked over to the three of them and looked out over the lake. "Wow! What a glorious day! Look at the blue sky reflecting on the water." She smiled. "Let's make doughnuts for breakfast."

"Yes, doughnuts! My favorite!" Danny pumped his fist in the air.

Doughnuts could be cooked in oil in a pan on the camp stove. No open fire was needed. Hank and Maddy worked together to prepare the special breakfast. Rachel helped. No one said much about the partially burned campsite.

Danny decided to go fishing by himself, though the prospects didn't look good. The rock face along the campsite slanted deep into the water. There were no weeds or underwater structures for good fish habitat. Nevertheless, like all boys hooked on fishing, Danny hoped for just one good strike. He cast for northern pike using a red-and-white daredevil attached to a long leader. Back and forth he worked the shoreline, casting out as far as his line would reach, letting the daredevil sink deep before reeling it in. For nearly an hour he cast and reeled, cast and reeled, each time coming up empty—not as much as a nibble.

"Breakfast!" Maddy called from up above him in the campsite.

"Okay, I'll be right there." Danny sent the red-and-white spoon out over the sky-blue water one last time. Plop—it broke the smooth surface and began its descent. Just as he started to reel it in, the fish hit hard, taking line out. Slowly he took up the slack; then with a snap of his rod he sunk the hook. Sixty feet out on the lake the small northern jumped with a quick splash of its tail. Danny played the skinny fish for a few minutes, then pulled it into shore.

Up close he discovered a northern pike like he had never seen before. Perhaps because it was such a young fish, the scales along its sides reflected a beautifully iridescent, multi-colored quality—light greens and yellows, pinks and blues. It looked to Danny like some kind of a magical fish, even though he knew it was just a small northern. He thought to call to his family, but decided to keep this catch to himself. Carefully, he detached the treble-hook and released the remarkable fish back into the water, watching it disappear into the depths of the lake.

"Come on, Danny!" Maddy called again.

Up in the campsite Danny found a stack of warm cinna-mon-sugared doughnuts piled high on a plate. Maddy and Rachel and Hank had already started eating. "Umm... Umm... my favorite." He picked up a doughnut in one hand and a cup of orange juice in the other.

"What'd you catch down there?" Hank asked.

"Just a snake northern." Danny didn't know how to explain the fish's mysterious beauty.

"Well, we have about seven or eight miles of paddling ahead of us to reach Rebecca Falls, with just one little portage into McAree Lake." Hank spread the map out for Rachel to see. "We might as well all wear our swimsuits. It feels like it's gonna' be a hot one."

"Don't forget the sunscreen," Maddy added, "and we should filter twice our usual amount of drinking water."

An hour later the campers were again on their way, heading south. Maddy wore her garden hat and her hospital scrubs over her swimsuit to prevent sunburn. Danny, Rachel and Hank all paddled in swimsuits and T-shirts. Danny and his mother took the lead down Minn Lake, with Maddy paddling stern in the Old Town. They skirted a densely wooded

island en route to the McAree Lake portage. Huge white pines leaned out over the water. As they rounded the island Danny spotted the white head of a large bald eagle against the dark pine branches high up in the tallest tree. He stopped paddling and pointed upward without speaking. Both canoes glided silently in the shadow of the island, Hank and Maddy steering. Rachel reached for her camera just as the great bird swooped down from its perch and crossed the water low in front of them. Click, click, click—she snapped off three pictures. "I got it," she whispered excitedly, as if talking out loud would matter. The eagle, light as air, its white tail glistening in the sunlight, rose up again and disappeared over the tree line to the west.

"Good job, bird-girl!" Hank splashed her lightly with his paddle.

The portage lay just ahead. With dry personal packs and two-thirds of the food consumed from the food pack, the campers made quick work of the easy fourteen rods. McAree Lake stretched north to south before them—a six-mile paddle directly into the sun, now high in the sky in front of them. Maddy slathered on more sunscreen and passed the bottle of lotion to Danny. He was now handling stern duty in the Old Town. They were in no particular hurry and the paddling was easy—no rescue effort into wind and waves—no night paddle—no beaver dams. Gliding side-by-side across the glass-like surface of the lake, the two canoes left perfect v-shaped wakes trailing behind them.

Far up ahead, Danny sighted a small motor boat crossing in front of them. "I thought this was a non-motorized lake... no motorboats?"

"The Lac La Croix Band has an agreement with the Canadian government." Hank knew his Ontario history. "The Quetico Park is land that the tribe gave up in a treaty back in the eighteen hundreds. But the people living at the First Nation community still need to make a living. Some work as fishing guides. So, the park allows a few fishing guides each day to work certain lakes within the park. They can use small fishing boats with ten-horsepower motors."

"Do you think we'll run into John Waterman?" Rachel asked.

"I don't know, Rachel." Hank shrugged his shoulders. "I don't know if John Waterman works as a fishing guide or just hauls canoes with his big boat."

"I'd like to see him again."

"Why, Rachel?"

"Because he looks just like you. You could pass as twin brothers."

"I don't think so, bird-girl. I don't think so."

Rachel and Maddy were paddling bow across from each other in the separate canoes. Maddy looked over at Rachel and gave her the raised-eyebrow signal, as if to say, enough already with the John Waterman questions. Rachel shut up.

Hank slowed the Seliga, checking the map and taking a compass reading. For a long while no one talked. Then Maddy stopped paddling. "I need some water." She reached for the water bottle under her seat. Danny could tell that she was already suffering in the heat. Hank and Rachel didn't seem to mind the sun. Their skin just got darker and darker. Danny could handle about half a day's worth. But the blond, fair-skinned members of the family, Maddy and Michael, burned red as fire if they didn't cover up, wear hats and use sunscreen. There was no place to hide on the big lake, no shelter, no shade, and the sunlight was intensified as it reflected off the water. Maddy would have to endure as best she could.

About halfway down the lake, Hank pointed out the McAree Rapids set back in a bay along the western shore-line—rumbling whitewater. "Let's move together for a float-ing TL." He drew the Seliga next to the Old Town and threw a short rope to Maddy in the bow. She tied the two bow thwarts together and Hank tied the two stern thwarts togeth-er. This formed a sturdy pontoon boat. "Danny and I can keep us moving straight. Here, Maddy, make a tent for your-self." Hank passed her a compact foil survival blanket.

"Thank you." Maddy turned around on her seat, faced backwards and pulled the foil blanket over her shoulders and head with the silver side of the blanket reflecting the sun. "Ahhh... it feels good to get out of the sun for just a minute. Turn around, Rachel, and help me fix TL."

Rachel turned around in her seat, too, facing Hank. Together she and her mother found the trail lunch bag and bottles of bug juice. Carefully they portioned out the quick energy food. Then they used the flat blade of Maddy's paddle to pass the sierra cups back to Hank and Danny. Spontaneously, floating out in the middle of McAree Lake on the hottest of all summer days yet, the Foresters looked at each other and raised their cups in a toast, "Foresters leave no trace!" They all smiled; perhaps, Danny thought, at how silly this must have looked—a family of four dressed in boots and swimsuits, life jackets and funny-looking hats. But he didn't care how geeky he looked out here, as long as Julie Tucker was back in Ohio.

"I wonder if we'll ever hear from the Tuckers?" he asked, looking at his mother.

"I'm sure we will," Maddy reassured him.

"You mean, you wonder if you'll ever hear from smooch-face Julie Tucker?" Rachel couldn't keep her mouth shut.

"That's it, brat! You're toast!" Danny rolled to his right, out of the stern seat and into the lake, swimming under the canoes. In a few seconds, his head popped up next to Rachel. She screamed and reached across for her mother, but that didn't stop Danny from furiously splashing his mouthy little sister.

"Hey! Hey! Hey!" Hank yelled, half laughing, half scolding. Then he, too, decided to go for a swim and rolled to his left into the lake. He splashed Danny, laughing, and Danny splashed him back. Then little Rachel stood up and jumped over the side, landing with a cannonball splash nearly on top of Danny.

"Oh, well, I might as well join you." Maddy dove in, scrubs and all.

The cold lake water felt great up against the burning heat of the sun. With the splashing stopped they floated like a pod of freshwater whales for another half an hour until they had cooled enough and it was time to move on. Hank helped Rachel into the bow of the Seliga, then he pulled himself into the stern. Maddy and Danny found their way back into the Old Town and untied the ropes connecting them with Hank and Rachel's canoe. Water dripped off of everyone into the bottoms of the boats, but the hot sun would soon dry them, even Maddy in her wet scrubs.

"We're about three miles from Rebecca Falls." Hank repositioned his map and compass. "We should be there in an hour or so."

A mile and a half later the lake narrowed into a deep channel marked as the Namakan River on the map. Upstream —the current ran against the paddlers, and for the first time all day, they had to put some effort into their paddling. Two groups of campers passed them heading north. Hopefully, this meant there would be less competition for campsites that night on Iron Lake.

Beautiful Rebecca Falls split around an island like Twin Falls. The portage, maybe thirty rods, ran across the island alongside the southern channel of the falls. At the landing below the falls, a Quetico Park canoe ranger in a green uniform had set up a checkpoint. The Foresters pulled easily up to a flat, dock-like rock.

"Good afternoon, folks. May I see your park permit?" The ranger was a short, stocky man, built like a voyageur. He helped them land and unload their canoes. Hank opened his rucksack and produced the proper papers. "I see you are Canadian, aye."

Hank nodded. "Is there a problem?"

"No, not as long as you have a camp stove. I'm here to tell you that the fire ban in the Quetico is now total. No open fires are allowed anywhere at anytime." Then he produced a red ink stamp and stamped the Forester's permit with big red letters—NO OPEN FIRES ALLOWED.

"What about the U.S. side?" Hank asked.

"Those crazy Americans are still allowing fires from seven until midnight." He handed the Hank his papers. "If I had it my way we'd close both parks down. This place is a tinderbox. We've had no rain for a month. I'm telling people to leave... go home. One night of heat lightning and we'll be fighting twenty fires at once." The ranger shook his head. "You folks be careful, aye."

"We will. We're very experienced campers." Hank tried to reassure the nervous ranger. Then he flipped up his Seliga.

Maddy and Danny had already flipped up the Old Town, but this time Danny would carry the canoe. He followed the trail along the sloping south channel of the falls, barely a trickle now compared to its usual volume of water. The trail led out of the shadows below the falls uphill to a sunny rock landing at Iron Lake. Here was where the summer heat hit them hardest. It must have been nearly a hundred degrees— an unheard of temperature for the northwoods.

Maddy wilted in the intense heat, her face scarlet red. "I need two things... some water... and to get out of the sun." She sat down in the shade of a scraggly cedar.

"Rachel, get some water for your mother. Danny, help me load the canoes." Hank barked out orders. "I have an idea. We can't just sit here out in the open. We have to get to the first campsite we can find." He pored over his map. "Come on!" Next he walked Maddy into the water and helped her into the bow compartment of the Seliga, sitting as a duffer. He handed her a bottle of water and covered her with the survival blanket, foil side out against the sun. "Drink!" He ordered. "Rachel, you paddle bow in Danny's canoe."

Hurriedly they raced out onto Iron Lake, looking for the first available campsite. Hank paddled alone with Maddy, duffing underneath her silver sun-shield. Rachel paddled harder than she had ever paddled before in the bow of the

Old Town. Luckily, a Forest Service campsite on the shaded north side of an American island appeared not far from the falls. They landed and helped Maddy up into the campsite, sitting her in the shade of a huge, fire-scarred red pine, like the one Bill Tucker had slept under. Hank threw a wet towel across her shoulders and pulled off her boots. Rachel and Danny filtered more water. A few minutes later, she was smiling self-consciously at all the attention from her worried family. "I'm okay. I'm okay. I just needed to get out of the sun. Thank you."

"Whew, you had us worried." Rachel hugged her mother.

"You better take it easy tonight." Hank's voice expressed genuine concern. He held her hand. It was the second time in two days that Danny had witnessed such a demonstration of affection between his parents. He liked what he saw. He had not liked their fighting earlier in the summer.

After a dinner of Hudson Bay stew, bannock and chocolate pudding, the four dusty campers took an evening swim, floating in their life jackets thirty feet out from the rocky shoreline. Maddy had recovered from her sunstroke.

"The only thing I really miss when we're camping is the refrigerator... being able to open the fridge door and find something cold to drink... like milk or juice." Danny stuck the toes of his boots out of the water.

"Well, in two more days we'll be back in refrigerator land." Hank sounded unenthusiastic about the prospect of returning to civilization.

"I miss Mike." Rachel spoke from the heart.

Danny missed Mike, too, for a lot of reasons, but especially if they were camped in a "tinderbox," and a forest fire came roaring at them, it would be great to have a warrior-firefighter like Mike at their side. He remembered his Mike-on-fire dream.

"Who misses Mike?" Everyone turned to the voice coming from a canoe that had silently sneaked up on them.

"Michael!" Maddy exclaimed. "It's Michael!"

It was big Mike, paddling with a young woman in an aluminum canoe that read U.S. FOREST SERVICE on the side. They drifted into shore as Hank, Maddy, Rachel and Danny scrambled out of the water.

"What are you doing here?" Hank asked, a wide grin of amazement on his face.

Mike and the young woman stepped out of the 'lumi. Mike tied the bow to a cedar tree with a length of rope, letting the canoe float in the shallows. They were both wearing green Forest Service T-shirts with khaki trail shorts and boots. Mike had let his beard grow out. Danny spotted a backpack fire extinguisher, the kind filled with water, lying in the canoe. A firefighter's hoe-like tool, called a pulaski, leaned against the fire extinguisher.

"They sent our crew to check on campsites in the Boundary Waters. We're camped on Lac La Croix, across from the pictographs. We volunteered to check the campsites on Iron Lake, making sure people were putting their fires dead out, looking out for lightning strikes. Besides, I told you I'd meet you on Iron Lake. So, here I am... here we are." Mike smiled at his partner. "This is Kari Knutson, firefighter extraordinaire."

The young woman, blond, athletic-looking, stepped up on shore. "Hello, good to meet you." She spoke with a slight Scandinavian accent.

Everyone hustled to change into dry clothes. Hank and Danny pulled on their cotton sweat suits. Rachel wore a pair of red pajamas. Maddy found a clean set of hospital scrubs. They hung their swimsuits and towels up to dry in the night air, then gathered around Mike and Kari Knutson at the fire pit. They were drinking hot cocoa poured from Hank's coffee pot sitting on the fire grate. Mike spoke up. "Well, you guys look none the worse for wear. How's your trip been so far?"

"You wouldn't believe us if we told you." Danny shook his head. "We had to save this family from Ohio who swamped in the middle of Lady Boot Bay. The dad had a heart attack."

"No way," Mike questioned Danny's report. But Hank and Maddy both nodded their heads.

"Yeah, and Danny has a girlfriend and Dad has a twin brother and Mom almost died from sunstroke today," Rachel blurted out her version of events, sitting next to her big brother.

Mike laughed. "Wow, you have had a big trip." He put his arm around Rachel.

"It's all a very long story." Hank poured everyone another cup of cocoa. "We saw the smoke from the Crane Lake fire. Tell us about it."

"Not much to tell." Mike sipped his cocoa. "It got a little hairy at times, with that south wind, but we got it under control the third afternoon. The Canadian water-bombers saved us."

"Well, there's a little more to the story than that; wouldn't you say, Michael?" Kari turned toward Mike's family. "Mike's a hero. He saved the lives of five other firefighters, including me."

"It was just luck." Mike shook his head, looking into the campfire.

"It was a lot more than luck. It was courage and leadership and quick-thinking."

"Tell us the story," Rachel begged.

"It's no big deal," Mike brushed her off.

But Kari Knutson was eager to report. She looked right at Rachel, sitting across from each other on campsite logs. "On our second day of fighting the fire, we thought we had it knocked down with the help of the American water bombers.

Most of the crew stayed back to cut a firebreak into the woods straight west from Crane Lake. Mike led a crew of six with water packs back toward the stunted flame front, looking for hot spots. I was with him. Suddenly, that mean south wind kicked up. And before we knew it, we were surrounded by flames, crowning overhead... sparks flying everywhere... burning branches falling... pine trees exploding... smoke. It was unbelievably hot... very, very hot... and very frightening."

Kari looked to Hank and Maddy and Danny. Rachel listened, wide-eyed. "But Mike kept his cool. He ordered us to drop everything except our fire shelters. Then he led us into a swamp, where we did the shake 'n' bake thing. The fire jumped over us. Not a scratch on anybody." She put her arm around Mike's shoulder. "Thanks again, big guy."

Hank shook his head. "That's our Mike."

"Kinda' makes up a bit for what happened in Utah, I guess." Mike looked at both of his parents. Danny sensed that his angry, restless big brother felt more at peace with himself this night.

"What an amazing story." Maddy stood up and checked the back of her older son's neck to see how his Utah burns had healed. "How long can you two stay? Overnight?"

"Nah, we should be heading back, over Bottle Portage to Lac La Croix. Our crew will be looking for us to return before dark. I just wanted to make sure you guys were okay in this high fire danger area." Mike stood up. "How many nights before you head home?"

"Just one more night." Danny answered. "I'm hoping we'll camp near Bear Island tomorrow night."

"All right, then. We might see you tomorrow on Lac La Croix. Tonight, I plan to stand lookout from Warrior Hill... watching for fires." Mike set his cup on a fire pit rock.

"Me, too." Kari smiled and set her cup on the rock next to Mike's cup.

Everyone walked with them down to the shoreline. As they passed the red canoe Mike noticed the fiberglass patch on its belly. "What happened?" He ran his hand over the wound.

"Lake-shark," Hank explained. "We'll stop in Ely on the way home and drop it off at Joe Seliga's workshop. I'll have him replace the cracked ribs and put a new skin on her."

"Good idea." Mike gave Maddy and Rachel a hug, then untied the 'lumi. He and Kari climbed in the canoe and paddled off, waving, toward Bottle Portage. They would have about an hour of light to make it back to their crew camped on Lac La Croix.

Mike's family watched until they were out of sight around a peninsula, then turned away. As they turned, Danny noticed the exchange of smiles and raised eyebrows between his parents. Perhaps they were remembering their first summer together in the Boundary Waters? He didn't ask them this question.

. . .

The air had cooled a bit with the setting sun. Strangely, no mosquitoes appeared. So, with no one especially eager to head into the tent, they sat quietly around a small campfire. Before long the stars came out, and later—the Northern Lights.

"Look!" Rachel pointed. Streaks of red, yellow and green formed a wavy curtain of light above the tree line to the north. "What makes the Northern Lights?"

"Do you want the scientific answer or the First Peoples answer?" Hank asked.

"Both," Rachel answered.

"Help me." Hank looked to Maddy for the scientific answer.

Maddy smiled. "I don't know too much about it, but I think the Northern Lights and the Southern Lights occur when solar wind hits the Earth's magnetic fields. This creates a powerful electrical charge that lights up the sky. If we were up in the space shuttle, we would see that the curtain of light we're looking at is actually a circle of light above the North Pole."

"Thank you, Dr. Madeline..." Hank smiled back at his partner, "for that astute answer." He looked up at the night sky. Rachel sat closer. "The Eskimos and Aleuts, the northern First Peoples, have a number of different ideas about the Aurora Borealis. Some believe they are the spirits of the dead lighting the way for newly departed souls to cross over from this world to the other world. Some believe the lights can heal sickness. Lots of people think you can call the lights closer to you by whistling to them."

"What does your tribe believe?" Rachel asked her father in earnest.

Hank paused, still looking up into the colorful sky. "Rachel, honey, I don't really know what tribe I'm a part of, so I don't know the answer to that question."

Danny thought again about the resemblance between John Waterman and his father. *Maybe my dad belongs to John Waterman's band of Ojibwe people, the Lac La Croix First Nation?* he asked himself. But he didn't say anything or give Maddy and Rachel the raised-eyebrow sign. He liked his father's First Peoples answer. Tomorrow, he wondered, would he like his father's answer to his request to camp alone on Bear Island?

Hank stood up and walked to the edge of the lake, whistling softly up into the northern night sky. Maddy and Rachel joined him, whistling softly, too. Danny stood back and watched. Slowly, ever so slightly it seemed, the shimmering curtain of light moved closer.

chapter nine

BEAR ISLAND SOLO

After breakfast the next morning, Danny, Rachel and Hank set out in the Seliga to explore Curtain Falls. Bigger than either Twin Falls or Rebecca Falls, Curtain Falls poured east to west from Crooked Lake into Iron Lake. The Foresters planned to head west that day, back to Lac La Croix. But because Rachel and Danny had never seen the big waterfalls to the east of their campsite, Hank wanted to show it to them. Maddy decided to stay at the campsite to pack up their gear. Besides, she said she wanted to stay out of the sun as long as she could, even though a thin haze of cloud cover had moved in overnight.

Approaching the falls from downstream, Hank gasped in astonishment at what he saw. "Man, what happened!" Mighty Curtain Falls appeared a fraction of its usual size. Where a deep, rumbling rapids usually flowed, a wide expanse of grayish-colored boulder-field rock lay exposed to the sky on either side of a narrow channel of blue water. Sun-

bleached driftwood logs jutted helter-skelter amongst the rocks. The dry, hot summer had reduced the famous landmark to this diminished condition.

To reach the portage landing below the falls, Hank and Danny paddled hard upstream against a wide v-slick of water rushing at them between two huge boulders. Danny paddled bow with Hank in the stern. "Ooo... that was a little scary." Rachel looked back at the v-shaped slick from her duffer seat. Hank gave her his how could you ever doubt your father's canoeing ability look. He and Danny two-manned the canoe out of the lake and set it down alongside the portage path.

"Follow me." Danny raced excitedly up the portage path, eighty-eight rods.

"Wait for me." Gripping her camera and her Birder's Ear, Rachel couldn't keep up. She dropped back to walk with her father, who was taking his time, limping a bit. They could hear the rumbling water off in the distance.

At the top of the portage, Crooked Lake stretched as far as Danny could see to the east. Its green waters slid effortlessly over the edge of the falls, funneled into a pounding shaft of whitewater for the initial ten-foot drop, then churned down a fifty-foot slope of rock before flowing west as a rapids into Iron Lake. In the dry weather conditions, the mist off the falls seemed to evaporate immediately, providing little in the way of drought relief to the thirsty forest.

Hank and Rachel caught up with Danny. "Not too close, now." Hank held Rachel's hand. They stood on the American side, looking across to Canada. Two other groups of campers were exploring the rocks below the falls. Hank sat down on a driftwood log. "Once, when I was guiding for camp, I fell over Curtain Falls."

Danny looked at his father, unbelieving.

"It's true. I was horsing around on the rocks, right about where you're standing. One minute I was laughing, the next minute... tumbling over the falls. My campers had to pull me out with a rope."

"No way!" Danny laughed.

"That's close enough." Hank waved his adventurous son back from the edge of the roaring waterfalls. Danny threw a small log into the raging whitewater just to watch it tumble and roll down the rapids. Rachel snapped some pictures.

·   ·   ·

Back at the campsite, Maddy had their gear neatly packed. She had even loaded the two personal packs into the Old Town, floating next to shore. By this point, day seven of the trip, the Foresters had found their rhythm as a camping team. Everyone knew what to do without being told. In no time at all they were off again, gliding across the water, synchronizing the casual dip-swing of their paddles.

"How'd you like Curtain Falls?" Maddy asked Rachel as they paddled bow-to-bow. A light wind and the hazy sky cooled the summer heat from the day before.

"I liked it a lot, but I especially liked the part about Dad being swept over the falls and he had to shout to his campers to rescue him with a rope. Did he ever tell you that story?"

"Rachel, remember, I was the camp doctor when your father was on the trail. I used to pray he'd make it back in one piece. As I recall the Curtain Falls episode, he came off the trail with all the bandages from the first aid kit wrapped around his shins."

Rachel flashed her father a big smile. He shrugged his shoulders. "Stop talking and start paddling," he pretended to grouch at the blabbermouth.

A half an hour later, muddy Bottle Portage took them back to Lac La Croix near Warrior Hill. Danny wasn't sure where his parents planned to camp for their last night on the trail. Nothing had been said about his Bear Island request. When they reached the big lake, Maddy asked to paddle stern. She and Hank steered the canoes southward without any discussion about the route, as if they both knew exactly where they were going. After a while, Hank called across to Maddy in the stern of the Old Town. "There." He pointed towards a dark, hump-shaped island.

"What's over there?" Danny asked.

"Bear Island," Hank answered, sounding serious. Danny's heart jumped. Ten minutes later they pulled up in front of a campsite on the westernmost end of the island.

"Here you go, camper." Maddy stepped out of the green canoe and held it steady for her son. "You wanted to do a solo, well here's your chance."

"Really?" Danny looked first to his mother, then his

father. They both nodded.

"We'll be right over there." Hank pointed due west to a campsite with a steep rock face on a long, skinny island, not more than a quarter of a mile away. Bear Island was positioned off the eastern end of the long, skinny island, like the dot of an exclamation point.

"Everything you need is in here." Maddy pointed to the #2 Duluth pack. Then she lifted the other personal pack into the Seliga and climbed into the duffer seat. The Old Town would stay with Danny. "We'll pick you up in the morning."

Rachel took a picture of Danny standing in the water beside his canoe and pack. Then she threw him her pith helmet with the mosquito netting. "You might need this."

"Thanks," Danny finally remembered to say. "I... I'll be okay."

"We know." Maddy gave him her confident-mom look. Hank back-paddled and turned the Seliga to the west. With waves from his mother and sister, they were off, across the lake to set up their own campsite.

Wow, Danny thought to himself, *I wish Mike could see this.*

He hauled the pack and canoe up onto shore and quickly surveyed the rocky campsite. Then he took inventory of his food and equipment: one girl's pith helmet with mosquito netting; one green seventeen-foot Old Town wood-and-canvas canoe; one laminated wooden paddle with a pictograph of a bear painted on the blade; one personal floatation device; one #2 Duluth pack. He unbuckled the straps of the pack.

Inside, his mother had carefully placed everything he would need to survive the night alone on Bear Island. First, he pulled out his collapsible fishing rod, stored with the reel and tackle in a hard plastic case. Maddy had attached the fillet knife to the case with a wide rubber binder. Next, he found a water bottle full of bug juice and three plastic bags of food. The first bag contained his portion of trail lunch for the day. The second bag contained a packet of instant chicken noodle soup and a box of dried hash-brown potatoes for dinner. She had included a little container of cooking oil and two packets of cocoa. Danny understood that if he wanted more to eat that night, he was going to have to catch a fish. The third bag contained two voyageur bars and some dried fruit bits for breakfast. He set the bags aside.

For cooking, she had given him a small pot and small frypan from the cook kit, plus a knife, fork, spoon and some folded aluminum foil. He had his sierra cup hooked on the belt of his trail shorts. For sleeping, she had packed the kitchen tarp for a shelter, with a length of rope, his sleeping bag and sleeping pad. Below the sleeping bag, he found a towel, his blue sweat suit, rain jacket and campsite shoes. Finally, he pulled out his ditty bag. Inside the red nylon bag, he found his toothbrush, toothpaste, a bar of soap, six bandaids, a bottle of water purification tablets, Rachel's flashlight and Hank's binoculars. There was no axe, saw, shovel, stove, fishing net, water filter or matches.

Wait a minute, he thought to himself, *no matches?* Carefully, he sorted through his pile of gear—still no matches. And, he remembered, he had given his ten-in-one compass device, with its fire-starting magnifying glass, to Julie Tucker. In that moment, he understood the challenge that had been set before him. He could survive on a trail lunch, voyageur bars and dried fruit; but if he wanted to cook fish, potatoes, soup and cocoa, he'd have to start a fire without matches. Everything came down to fire.

He stood up with the binoculars and scanned the lake to the west. His mother, father and sister had landed on the eastern end of the skinny island. Their campsite sat much higher above the water than his site. He could see Hank carrying the red canoe up a trail to the right of the steep rock face and into the campsite. Maddy and Rachel stood on top of the rock looking back in his direction. No one waved. He turned away. Forgetting the fire question for now, it was time to explore the island.

Carefully, he repacked his food and equipment, except for the trail lunch and rope. He used the rope to string the pack from a long white pine branch overhanging the center of the campsite. Standing below the pack, he swatted the air above his head with his hands, like bear paws, to make sure it was high enough off the ground. With that task completed, he positioned the Old Town diagonally across the only tent site he could find. He would sleep under the canoe. But for now, he had the whole afternoon to hike about the island, collect firewood and go fishing.

A well-used trail led away from the campsite around the perimeter of the island. Danny followed the shoreline path behind twisted clumps of cedar trees leaning out over the water. Occasionally, looking inland, he would spot the black root wad of a windfall jack pine tree. He remembered how he used to think those dark root wads, from a distance, looked like black bears lurking in the forest. But he had overcome his fear of bears on last year's trip. Or had he? Maybe that was why he wanted to camp alone on Bear Island—to test his courage.

About halfway around the island the trail split in two. The main path continued along the shoreline. Another path, less obviously traveled, led toward the middle of the island. Danny paused for a moment, then turned inland, hiking uphill through a stand of thin birch trees. Their light green leaves rustled slightly in the afternoon breeze, as if to welcome him.

In their approach from the northwest, the island had appeared to be entirely tree-covered, but the stand of birch trees opened up to a small clearing and rock outcropping facing southeastwardly. It was as if some ice age giant had dropped a handful of two-ton boulders at that spot. The slabs of gray, lichen-covered granite leaned against each other at odd angles. Danny stopped there, sitting on a flat rock. He pulled his trail lunch out of his pocket. But soon, as he chewed on a piece of licorice, he noticed a putrid odor from behind him. He turned to survey the pile of square-cornered rocks at his back. Looking more closely, he discovered a cave-like opening in the center of the boulder pile.

The bad smell seemed to be coming from the opening in the rocks. Danny set his lunch down and picked up a stick. Slowly, he approached the cave, peering into its dark interior. The afternoon sun was at his back, so he could see partway into the hole. As his eyes adjusted to the light, he realized—he had discovered a bear den. Right there in front of him lay the rotting carcass of a black bear—perhaps a sickly old bear that had not survived the winter hibernation or the summer drought with its shortage of nuts and berries.

Danny poked at the sunken carcass with his stick. Maggots wiggled. The bear's big skull had already been stripped clean. Hunks of fur had fallen to the floor of the cave. A lone bear paw protruded from the mess near the front of the cave. Danny remembered the camper's motto—take only pictures, leave only footprints—but he couldn't resist the temptation. He reached into the cave and plucked a long bear claw off the end of the rotting paw. Then he stepped back, took a clean breath of air, and put the claw in his pocket.

Was this my bear, he wondered, *the bear I had stood up to in the campsite on last year's trip?* He used to have dreams of being chased by ferocious, angry bears. But on last September's trip with Mike and his father, he found the courage to stand up to a huge black bear that charged into their campsite one night. Since then, no more bear night-mares had haunted him. But it wasn't just that he had stood up to the bear, he had somehow communicated with the bear. They had understood each other. The next night, when the terrible thunderstorm hit their Kahshahpiwi campsite, the spirit of the bear came to Danny's aid, giving him the strength to move the fallen tree trunk off of the tent where Mike and Hank were trapped and injured. Perhaps this was why his parents had allowed him to camp alone on Bear Island—they understood his deep connection with the bear.

On his return hike, Danny collected an armload of firewood, pine knots included. Plus, he selected one sturdy straight stick and one slightly curved stick, each about two feet long. These he would use to make his fire, confident of success.

His boots and socks had dried while walking. Back at the campsite, he lowered the Duluth pack from the white pine and set about getting organized for the night. First, he fashioned a lean-to over the canoe for a tent. Next, he spread out his sleeping pad and bag under the canoe. He laid his sweat suit out on the sleeping bag next to Rachel's pith helmet. Without a mosquito net tent door, he might need his little sister's goofy-looking hat, with its netting, to keep the mosquitoes off his head during the night. Finishing that task, he set up a fire in the fire grate, ready to light at seven o'clock. Until then, he would fish off the rocks in front of the campsite.

Walleyes. Danny would fish hard for one dinner of walleyed pike, his favorite. Meticulously, he assembled his rod and reel, double-checking each connection. Then he sorted through his collection of Mepps spinners. He chose a shinny gold Mepps-3 with red and yellow feathers and a treble hook. The sun had shifted to the west, still partially hidden by the light cloud cover. He guessed it was four o'clock. He would have three hours before he could start a fire—plenty of time to catch a fish.

A toppled jack pine, angling into the water, offered promise. He cast out from shore, over and over, parallel to the
weathered tree trunk. Patience—fishing had taught him
patience. Mike had taught him how to tie fishing line knots,
and his father had showed him how to fillet a fish, but the
fishing itself had taught him patience. No luck casting.
Perhaps the sun was too high. Danny sat cross-legged on the
shoreline and replaced the spinner with a Lindy Rig, attach-
ing a floating plastic nightcrawler for bait. He cast the rig
next to the jack pine and let it sink. There was nothing to do
then but wait for a fish to start running with his line.

Reaching into the pocket of his trail shorts, he pulled out
his Swiss army knife and the treasured bear claw. The claw
was like a long, curved fingernail attached to a piece of bone
from the bear's hand-like paw. He opened up the awl tool on
the knife and carefully began drilling a hole through the
stubby bone-end of the claw. He would make himself a bear-
claw necklace, drilling carefully until the awl poked through
the other side of the bone. Then, inside his fishing kit he
found a thin red cord, used for a fish stringer. He cut a length
of the red cord and threaded it through the hole he had
drilled in the claw. To finish his creation, he tied the two
ends of the cord together and slipped the necklace over his
head. Forget the rules. He would keep the claw forever.

Zip—zip—zip—fishing line spun out of his reel. He
grabbed his pole, took up the slack, and with a quick snap,
set the hook. He had a fish! It dove and ran out line, then
zigzagged back and forth. Carefully, he played the lively
fish—perhaps his only chance for a full dinner that night.
Slowly, he wore it down and pulled it into the shallows
where he trapped it with his hands, like a bear, and flipped it
onto shore—a golden walleye, nice size, weighing perhaps
two pounds. Time for dinner.

He disassembled and packed away his collapsible rod and

reel. Instead of attempting to fillet the fish, he simply cut off the head and tail and gutted it, setting the fish guts on some shoreline rocks downwind from the campsite. Carefully wrapping his precious meal in a double-layer of the aluminum foil Maddy had packed for him, he planned to bake the fish in the hot coals of his campfire. But it was still too early to light a fire. In the meantime, he readied his pot and fry pan for cooking the soup and potatoes. It wasn't until he saw the firelight from his family's campsite that he figured it was seven o'clock. By now he was ravenous, but how to start a fire? Danny knew exactly how.

He had set aside his two fire sticks, one straight, one curved. With his knife he shaved the straight stick to a point on each end. Next, he took the lace from one of his boots, looped it twice around the middle of the straight stick and strung the lace tight across the curved stick, like a bow. The two sticks were positioned at a right angle to each other, with the bootlace looped around the middle of the straight stick. Mike had showed him this fire-starting method.

Then he found a narrow split log, flat on one side, and another chunk of wood, just the right size to fit in his hand. He used his knife again to carve out holes in each piece of wood, just big enough for the ends of the straight stick. Holding down the flat log with his feet in front of the fire grate, he put one end of the straight stick into the hole on the log. Then he held the stick straight up with the top end stuck in the hole in the smaller piece of wood he was gripping in his left hand. Lastly, he took the bow in his right hand and, fast as he could, sawed it back and forth. This motion spun the point of the straight stick very fast, down into the flat log, creating a friction. Soon enough, the wood started to smoke. Carefully, Danny nudged his birchbark tinder toward the smoking wood, blowing ever so slowly to add some oxygen.

Harder and harder he sawed his bow, like a mad fiddler making hot music. Fuel—heat—oxygen—all the ingredients for fire were at hand. Then poof! Just like that, just like Mike said it would happen, a small flame popped up from the smoking tip of the stick. Danny dropped his bow fire-starter and squatted above the delicate flame. Slowly, carefully, he added tinder, more and more tinder, until the fire took hold and he was able to push the flaming birchbark into the fire grate, beneath a pile of sticks. *Yes!* He pumped his fist and danced a little dance. *Fresh walleye tonight!*

In a few minutes he was eating. He had saved most of his bottle of bug juice for dinner and quickly devoured the instant soup while waiting for the potatoes to cook and the fish to bake. When the golden potato shreds were done on both sides, he tore open the hot foil surrounding his walleye meal—cooked to perfection, white, tender, succulent. Easily, he pulled the delicious meat from between fish bones and skin and piled it on his plate next to the potatoes. *Could life get any better than this for a thirteen-year-old boy from Minnesota?* Danny smiled to himself as he stuffed his mouth with forkfuls of food. A little chipmunk scurried in front of him, cheeks stuffed with food, too.

Sitting there, savoring his dinner, he remembered a book he had read last year in seventh grade—*My Side of the Mountain*—the story of a boy named Sam who lived off the land for a year by himself in a tree house in the Catskill Mountains. Maybe he could stay on Bear Island for a year, living off the land? He could make a shelter. He could catch fish. He could build fires. What else was there? If Mike's favorite place in all the Boundary Waters and Quetico Park was Warrior Hill, and Hank's favorite place was Lake Kahshahpiwi, then his special place would be Bear Island. For just a moment, he thought about hiding from his family when they came to pick him up in the morning. But night

would soon be upon him, and he needed to ready himself for the dark.

The sun dropped more quickly than he anticipated—a red disk through the clouds above the tree line to the west. The slight breeze that had blown all day had quieted. Hurriedly, he cleaned his dishes and packed away the rest of the trail food, deciding not to hang his pack. Keeping his fire small, he added only pine knots as the sun finally set. The pine resin burned hot, producing the most colorful of flames— shades of blue, green, red and purple. As he sat staring at the colors, sipping a cup of cocoa, the distinctive sound of Rachel's loon whistle drifted towards him from across the water to the west. In no time at all, her loon-kin answered her call with yet another wilderness symphony.

His fire burned low—red coals glowing. In the near dark- ness he soaked the ashes, making four trips back and forth to the lake to fill his water bottle and small cook kit pot. He left the last bottle full of water standing full for morning—three water purification tablets dissolving on the bottom. With his stomach full of fish and potatoes, and his bear-claw necklace around his neck, he was ready for sleep. All he had to do was make it through the night and eat breakfast in the morning to complete his island solo.

He used Rachel's flashlight to find his way to the makeshift tent. Setting his boots and socks by his head, he pulled on his sweat suit and crawled into his sleeping bag. A few mosquitoes buzzed beneath the canoe. Tying the drawstring of his hooded sweatshirt tight below his chin, his eyes closed shut as soon as his head touched his PFD pillow. Fast asleep, he never saw the first flashes of heat lightning, low in the night sky above the western horizon, heading towards Bear Island.

chapter ten

CHASING FIRE

Perhaps it was the mosquitoes that first woke him.
Danny groped in the dark for Rachel's pith helmet and
pulled the mosquito netting over his face. Falling back asleep,
he returned to his dreams. And later, closer to morning, his
old bear friend found him, nudging him with his snout, lick-
ing his face with his rough tongue. The dream seemed all too
real. Danny woke with a start, opening his eyes wide. He sat
up, looking across the lake, thinking that the light he saw on
the horizon was the sunrise. Was it morning already? Then
he remembered—he was facing west—the sun always rose in
the east. What was this reddish light to the west? He crawled
out of his sleeping bag and stood up. It was then that he realized—the island where his family had camped was on fire!

"Fire!" he screamed as loudly as he could—frantic in that
moment—heart pounding—adrenaline pumping. "Think," he
said to himself, "stop and think." Quickly, he pulled on his
trail shorts, boots and life jacket. Tearing down the lean-to,

he freed up the canoe. In a burst of strength, he flipped the Old Town up onto his shoulders and ran it into the lake, dropping it belly-down with a splash. "Paddle? Where's my paddle?" He raced back into the campsite and found his paddle leaning against a tree.

"Fire! Fire! Fire!" he yelled again and again, throwing himself into the stern of the canoe, hitting his strokes hard against the water, switching sides back and forth to keep running straight. "Fire! Fire! Fire!" No sign of life from his family—but the smoke and flames had not yet reached their campsite.

Vast Lac La Croix—the distance to the island was longer than he had imagined. Paddling alone—half the power of two. "Fire!" he screamed—voice already hoarse. Paddling in the near darkness, he raced against the racing fire with its crown of flames jumping treetop to treetop west to east across the island—heading directly toward his family's campsite.

The bow of the empty canoe rode too high out of the water with Danny in the stern. He should have sat more toward the center—a rookie mistake, but he had never paddled an empty canoe alone before. He gave up on screaming and concentrated on keeping control of the twisting canoe. Two hundred yards out, one-fifty, one hundred yards to go— then a slippery deadhead just below the surface—flipping the boat sideways—throwing the would-be rescuer into the cold water. "No!" he cried, slamming his fist on the swamped canoe.

Quick thinking—he stowed his paddle and started swimming, kicking with his boots on. He would swim the distance to the steep rock face of his family's campsite. *I can do this. It's just like they taught us in gym class. I can do this.* Stroke, breathe, stroke. *If Julie Tucker can swim with one arm, I can make it to that island,* he told himself. Fire in the west—a racing crown of flames—yellow sparks flying into the black night sky.

Stroke, breathe, stroke—arms aching—lungs bursting—
stroke, breathe, stroke—until at last the shoreline—solid
ground! "Fire!" Danny gasped, crawling on hands and knees
up the steep rock face—clawing his way to the top—black
smoke choking—red deer dashing—food pack swinging from
a rope. "Fire!" he yelled one last time.

Hank bailed out of the tent first, then Maddy with Rachel
screaming in her arms—flaming trees falling everywhere,
igniting the duff all around. Hank threw his rucksack at
Danny. "Get the paddles!" He yelled. "I got the canoe."

Danny dodged a fiery branch and grabbed the paddles
and life jackets. Maddy literally ran down the rock face with
Rachel in her arms and jumped into the lake. Danny followed, throwing the life jackets, pack and paddles to Rachel
and Maddy in the water. Hank flew off the rock with the red
Seliga on his shoulders—like a giant eagle—turning the canoe
onto its belly and screaming in pain just as he hit the water.

"Get in!" Eight arms and legs pulled and crawled at once.
Three paddle blades hit the water. Above them, the campsite
erupted into flames. "The food pack's on fire!" Hank looked
back at the red inferno. "The propane fuel canisters for the
stove will explode like a bombshell! Get under the canoe!
Hold your breath! Hang on! Here we go!" Maddy grabbed
Rachel. Danny grabbed the gunwale. Hank rolled the canoe
over in the water. Seconds later, four heads popped up into
the air pocket beneath the canoe.

KA-BOOM! KA-BOOM! The fuel canisters exploded,
throwing hot debris into the lake where it sizzled as it landed.
The frightened Foresters hugged, cried and prayed together
beneath the red canoe.

Then, incredibly, they heard two boat motors and the
sound of a man's voice calling out, "Yo! Anybody there?"

Hank stuck his head out from under the canoe. Danny

followed. "Hey! Over here! Over here!" Hank shouted. In a few seconds, Hank and Danny spotted the lighted bows of two U.S. Forest Service boats cutting through the smoke. It was Mike and his firefighting crew. "Mike! Over here!" Hank called again. "Get us outta' here!"

Mike steered toward his frightened family. By now, Maddy and Rachel had swum out from under the canoe. It was nearly dawn. Floating fifty yards out from the island, they could all still feel the heat from the fire, popping and cracking in the distance.

Mike pulled his boat up next to the overturned canoe. "We saw the fire and headed this way. Then we heard the explosions. Are you guys okay?"

"I either sprained or broke my ankle, but otherwise we're okay." Hank winced a bit as he talked.

Maddy spoke up, "Rachel's pretty cold in this water. We need to watch for shock."

"Give her to me." A dozen stalwart firefighters pulled the shivering Foresters into their boats—Maddy and Rachel into Mike's boat, Hank and Danny in with the others. Kari Knutson wrapped Rachel in a jacket.

The firefighters with Hank and Danny dragged the upside down Seliga over the gunwales of their boat. All the water drained out. Then they turned the canoe upright and slid it back into the lake, tying a rope to the bow to tow it with them. Behind them, the island burned hot, lighting up the pre-dawn sky.

"Where's the green canoe?" Mike asked, sounding more concerned about one of the Forester's cherished canoes than the fire at hand. Besides, the first island was lost to the fire. All they could do now was watch it burn and move in later to hose down the hot spots. Mike asked again, "Where's the Old Town?"

Danny pointed to the place where he had run into the

submerged log and capsized.

"Wait a minute," Mike questioned him, "are you telling us that you swamped out there and swam the rest of the way to that island?"

Danny nodded.

"And then you climbed that rock face, didn't you?"

He nodded again.

"Man, that makes you a Lac La Croix warrior." Mike smiled at his little brother.

No, Danny thought to himself, *you're the real family warrior. I just did what I had to do.*

Working together, the firefighters retrieved and re-floated the green Old Town. But just as they slid it back into the water, Mike pointed to the sky above Bear Island. "Look!" The west wind had picked up with the sunrise. Now, dozens of burning embers were drifting due east, towards Bear Island, dropping sparks from the sky like lighted match heads. "If Bear Island burns, the mainland is next, with almost nothing to stop this fire from spreading. Let's go!"

They motored at top speed toward Bear Island. Someone handed Danny a hardhat, a yellow fire shirt and pair of leather gloves. "You're a firefighter, now, kid."

"Okay." Danny nodded, a bit unsure of what this meant.

"I'll set up a first aid station," Maddy called out as they landed at Danny's campsite. She helped Hank limp to shore on a badly sprained ankle.

Hurriedly, the crew unloaded their equipment—hand-operated backpack fire extinguishers called backpack pumps, pulaski tools, chain saws and two gasoline-powered water pumps with hoses. Kari Knutson talked over a two-way radio, calling for help from the fire base camp in Ely. Now, burning embers were falling everywhere, igniting the duff.

"Attack this fire!" Mike barked out orders. "You, you and you, come with me." He pointed to three firefighters, Kari

Knutson among them. Together, they grabbed one of the gasoline-powered water pumps, two coils of fire hose and a can of gasoline. "We gotta' get to some open ground... someplace where we can make a stand." He looked directly at Danny.

"I know the way to a clearing in the center of the island." Danny had guessed Mike's question.

"How far inland from the shoreline?" Mike wanted to know.

"I don't know, maybe two hundred feet, or less." Danny shrugged his shoulders.

"Good enough!" Mike handed his brother a pulaski tool and a backpack pump. "Go! Lead the way!" But Danny hesitated, looking over at his mother and father.

Maddy yelled across the campsite. "Michael! What do you think you are doing?"

He yelled back. "We need him to lead us to the clearing in the middle of this island before it goes totally up in flames. If this island goes, the whole BWCAW might go... up in flames!"

Maddy paused, glaring at Mike. "You watch out for your little brother!" Then she gave her nod of approval. Hank nodded, too.

"If it gets too hot, we'll just jump in the lake," Mike called over his shoulder.

Danny took the lead, running breathlessly along the perimeter trail, more adrenaline pumping. The metal backpack pump full of water was as heavy as a food pack. The pulaski tool, part axe, part hoe, was also much heavier than it looked. His knuckles and knees were bleeding and stung from his crawl up the mini Warrior Hill. Sweat ran down his face from beneath his hardhat. But soon enough, he found the path to the clearing. "Here." When he reached the bear den birch tree trail, he stepped aside, nearly out of breath, and pointed uphill.

Mike and two of the firefighters passed him running. Mike carried a big chainsaw. The others carried backpack pumps and pulaski tools, along with the gasoline-powered water pump and hoses. "Come on!" Mike yelled. Danny followed his brother. Kari Knutson stayed by the shoreline to set up the water pump and attach the hoses.

In the middle of the island, the upper branches of a dry jack pine had already caught fire. Mike attacked the base of the tree with his chainsaw, dropping it onto the rocks with a crash. His crew used their backpack pumps to hose down the red-yellow flaming branches.

"Knock down those hot spots!" Mike shouted orders.

Danny hacked frantically at the smoldering duff with his hoe-like tool; but for every burning ember he smothered, three more dropped from the sky. Still wearing his trail shorts, he could feel the heat on his legs. He dropped his pulaski tool and began working the hand pump from his backpack, spraying lake water at the spreading flames. Harder and faster he worked—spinning—turning—chasing fire all around him—black smoke choking—flaming branches falling—trees exploding—burning Bear Island—until his pump ran dry. "Mike!" he screamed, looking around "What now?"

"Everybody head for the lake!"

The four firefighters ran from the flames, Danny in the lead, until wham!—he fell hard onto the rocky ground. Blood ran freely from his split lip, dripping down onto his yellow fire shirt. Staggering to his feet, he could feel the heat from the fire at his back. Just then he was hit with a spray of water—it was firefighter Knutson, running up the trail with a fire hose spraying water. She hosed him down. "Get to the lake!" she yelled.

Mike grabbed hold of the hose and he and Kari pulled it

up to the clearing, spraying water at the biggest of the flames. The other two firefighters each grabbed one of Danny's arms and ran with him down to the shoreline next to where the gasoline-powered pump was drawing water out of the Lac La Croix. Standing knee-deep in the lake, they refilled their backpack pumps with water. Neither firefighter seemed to notice Danny's split lower lip.

"Come on, kid, we're not done yet. We still need you." One of the firefighters lifted Danny's pump onto his back— just as heavy the second time around. Danny sucked in a deep breath of fresh air from off the lake; and as best he could, still dripping blood, he followed the two men up the trail to the smoky clearing.

Up top was a grim scene. Mike and Kari were fighting a loosing battle—not enough hose to reach the worst of the fire. Danny soon emptied his backpack pump and dropped it off his shoulders. The heat off the flames felt more intense than ever. In a flash, he remembered his Mike-on-fire dream. He glanced back towards the lake, the cool wet wonderful lake, making sure he had an escape route. Then he picked up his pulaski and began to hack at the burning embers dropping from the sky onto the duff all around him—lost in the smoke—tasting blood—sweat pouring off his face blackened face—spinning—turning—crying out—"Mike! Mike!"

"Look out! Everyone take cover!" It was Mike—tackling Danny—rolling with him near the rocky entrance of the bear den—his loud voice drowned out by the engine roar of two Canadair CL-215 water-bombers, tracking low over Bear Island, dropping twenty-eight hundred gallons of water onto the fire. Whoosh! Whoosh! In an instant the fire was extinguished—only smoke and sizzle left behind—no flames.

"Yahoo!" Mike and his crew jumped for joy. Danny smiled self-consciously as Mike's firefighters all shook his hand. Kari Knutson slapped him on the top of his hardhat. It was then that Mike first noticed the bear claw around Danny's neck. "I see you've been hanging out with your bear again." He pointed to the necklace.

Danny nodded, and knew immediately what he must do. Take only pictures, leave only footprints. With his Swiss army knife, he cut the red cord and pulled his precious bear claw off the string. Carefully, he placed it back where he had found it—in the bear's den. But he vowed to return one day to Bear Island, his special place in the wilderness.

. . .

Back at the bustling campsite, everyone cheered and welcomed the hilltop firefighters. Heroes. They had slowed the spread of the fire enough to allow time for the water-bombers to knock down the biggest flames. Two more crews had arrived by floatplane. Twenty firefighters in all were working the fire now, using four lakeside water pumps to hose down the hot spots, smoldered duff and smoking tree stumps.

Amidst the chaos, the five members of the Forester family found each other. First Maddy examined Danny's split lip, shaking her head. "Looks like you won't be kissing Julie Tucker for a while," Rachel chirped up.

"Shut up," Danny pretended to growl at bird-girl. It was then he realized how much blood had run down the front of his shirt, and how much he smelled like fish guts, lake water, wood smoke and sweat.

But this didn't matter to anyone. Hank rose to his feet on a crutch made from a canoe paddle. The Forester family stood in a circle by the U.S. Forest Service fire grate, arms around each others' shoulders. Mike motioned for Kari Knutson to join them, and they welcomed her, too. Later that day, they would paddle over to the fire-blackened island where Hank and Maddy and Rachel had camped. There, they would retrieve what they could from the ashes—Hank's old cook kit—Maddy's reflector oven. But for now, they bowed their heads in gratitude. "We are grateful…" Danny began the prayer, but that was all anyone could say. "We are grateful."

THE END

ABOUT THE AUTHOR AND ILLUSTRATOR

Earl Fleck has camped for more than 30 years in the BWCAW and Quetico Wilderness regions. A psychologist in private practice and an investigator for the Minnesota State Attorney General's Office, he lives with his family near Minneapolis, Minnesota. His first book, *Chasing Bears: A Canoe Country Adventure*, was published by Holy Cow! Press in 1999.